PUFFIN BOOKS

MY SECOND BIG STORY-BOOK

Parents of young children need a wide range of good stories to satisfy their insistent appetites, and this need is splendidly met in Richard Bamberger's collections of fairy tales.

The stories in this second selection are rather longer than those in the first book, and are intended for children who are beginning to read, but the variety and interest are the same. As well as old favourites like Cinderella and Puss in Boots, it includes many less well-known stories from all over the world, like the shrewd and funny Master Money and Madam Fortune (from Spain) and the enchanting Princess under the Earth (from Greece). These are stories which parents will enjoy telling, and which children will remember with pleasure for the rest of their lives.

For readers and listeners of five and over.

Also available in Puffins:

My First Big Story Book
My Third Big Story Book

Richard Bamberger

My Second Big Story-Book

Translated by James Thin
Illustrated by Emanuela Wallenta

Puffin Books

Puffin Books, Penguin Books Ltd,
Harmondsworth, Middlesex, England
Penguin Books, 625 Madison Avenue, New York,
New York 10022, U.S.A.
Penguin Books Australia Ltd, Ringwood,
Victoria, Australia
Penguin Books Canada Ltd,
2801 John Street, Markham, Ontario, Canada L3R 1B4
Penguin Books (N.Z.) Ltd,
182–190 Wairau Road, Auckland 10, New Zealand

Mein zweites grosses Märchenbuch first published 1962
This translation first published by Oliver & Boyd 1962
Published in Puffin Books 1974
Reprinted 1975, 1977, 1979, 1980, 1982

Made and printed in Great Britain by
Hazell Watson & Viney Ltd,
Aylesbury, Bucks
Set in Linotype Pilgrim

Contents

Dear Parents

Your child is still at that happy time of life when he receives nearly all his books from his parents. If you will think for a moment that the impressions and experiences of childhood are of decisive and lasting importance for the rest of one's life, you will immediately realize the great responsibility you have in selecting reading material for your child.

This responsibility may well prompt you to ask me whether fairy-tales are in fact the right spiritual material for your child. I am well aware that strong objections have been raised to the fairy-tale: it puts too great a strain on the child's powers of imagination; it is not true to life; it brings the child face to face at too early an age with superstition, terror and even brutality.

Other scholars and teachers, on the contrary, maintain that no child ought to grow up without fairy-tales. The fairy-tale is filled with a wealth of magical vistas and with the innocence of the child's soul, said Herder. It is the first faint gleam of poetry to touch the growing sensibility of the child, said Scherer. Fairy-tales are told so that the child's earliest thoughts and emotions may awaken and flourish in their pure and gentle light, said Grimm.

Modern psychologists are of the opinion that fear and horror are a part of life itself. In the fairy-tale the child not only experiences this fear, but learns how to overcome it. The hero of the fairy-tale is a simplified image of man on his journey through life, a journey which inevitably leads him through darkness and difficulty. But on the way the hero battles against the powers of evil and returns victorious to the world of goodness and light. In this way the fairy-tale increases the child's confidence in his own strength, and he knows that he can overcome evil.

We stand in the middle of life, and we know that every situation has two sides to it. Where there is light, there is inevitably deep shadow. The truth often lies between the two. In presenting fairy-tales to children we must never forget that there are enormous differences between one child and another. That is why many educationists hold that fairy-tales ought to be read to children only by their parents, as it is the parents who know the child best.

This point of view, however, fails to take into account the fact that the family circle is often less close nowadays than it was in the past. The fairy-tale is no longer transmitted orally from generation to generation, and parents of today often stand in need of help for their story-telling.

Here then is the purpose of this collection of stories. It is my hope that it will lighten the parents' burden of responsibility in their selection of stories. From many thousands of fairy-tales I have selected those in which the powers of evil are shown in retreat, and truth and beauty, goodness and light stand well to the fore.

The beneficial influences of the fairy-tale become valid only when the powers of evil are truly overcome in the child's mind and leave no dark shadows behind. The reader must always be able to identify himself easily with the hero on his way to salvation, liberation and victory.

If I may be permitted to give you one more piece of advice, it is this. Do not leave your child to struggle alone with his dreams and experiences of darkness and light. Even if he has been going to school for some years, you can still do a great deal to help him if you will make a point of sparing the time to read or tell him stories, and if you will show patience and interest when he wants to tell or read *you* a story, or to talk it over with you.

Do not smile or be sceptical if my advice strikes you as being old-fashioned. Modern psychology points to a great many instances where a real interest and participation in every concern of the child has proved to be the foundation of a successful education and upbringing. The fairy-tale is very much the child's concern. Make a bold and realistic attempt to enter into the fairy-tale world with your child. Soon you will find yourselves looking forward to those hours when the magical world of fantasy unites the family in a vivid and exciting experience.

RICHARD BAMBERGER

Dear Children

Here is your *Second Big Story-Book*. I know that many of you will have been looking forward to it, because you have read the *First Big Story-Book* several times already from cover to cover.

Many of you, of course, can read perfectly well for yourselves by now, but I expect your teacher still reads to you at school from time to time, and I know you like your parents to tell you stories. If they are feeling lazy and you want to hear a story, ask them to read one of the tales from this book.

If there is any story which you like particularly, read it over and over again. Quite suddenly the story will become so alive and real to you that you will want to tell it to others. Your parents and your brothers and sisters will listen to you. I am sure you would like to hear them say, 'That was a lovely story – and how well you told it!'

Have you ever tried acting a story? It is great fun, either at school or at home – or even in the garden. Read your favourite story several times until you know it almost by heart, and then try to act it with your friends. One of you can be the prince, another the wolf, or the giant, or the princess, or whatever else you need for your story.

If you like drawing, particularly with crayons, why don't you start to make your own drawings for these stories? As you read them, I am sure you will think of all sorts of new and exciting ideas for pictures.

In this way all your story-books will give you a great deal of pleasure – in listening to the stories, in reading and telling them yourself, in acting them, and in drawing pictures for them.

Are you ever bored? Well, you won't be with this story-book. There are too many stories in it for you to have the chance!

Rapunzel

For a very long time a man and his wife had wanted a child, but in vain. At last the woman began to hope that God was going to grant her dearest wish.

Now there was a tiny window at the back of their house, from which they could see a splendid garden, full of the rarest flowers and the strangest herbs. But this lovely garden was surrounded by a high wall, and no one dared to go in. It belonged to an old lady who was a powerful witch, and everyone feared her.

One day the woman was standing at her window, looking down into the garden below, and she saw a new bed of the most beautiful green herbs. They looked so fresh and appetizing that she felt a great longing to taste them. As the days went by she longed more and more for the bright green herbs, and when she realized that she would never taste them, she grew pale and wretched and wasted away.

Her husband was frightened and asked, 'What is the matter, dear wife?'

'Alas,' she replied, 'if I do not have some of those lovely green herbs from the garden behind our house, I am sure I shall die!'

The man was in despair, for he loved his wife dearly, and he made up his mind to fetch some herbs, no matter what the cost. When night began to fall he climbed the high wall into the witch's garden, plucked a handful of herbs, and took them to his wife. She was delighted and immediately made them into a salad, which she ate with great appetite.

But she enjoyed them so much that the next day she wanted the herbs more than ever, and she gave her husband no peace until he climbed the wall a second time. No sooner had he dropped down on the other side than he found himself face to face with the witch.

'How dare you come into my garden and steal my plants,' she said, her eyes flashing in anger. 'I'll see that you pay dearly for this!'

'Alas!' he replied in terror. 'Please forgive me this time. My need was great, for my wife would have died without your herbs.'

'Very well,' said the witch. 'If it is as you say, you may take all the herbs you want, but on one condition: I must have your baby, as soon as it is born. I shall be a good mother to it and take great care of it.'

In his fear the man agreed to everything. When the baby was born the witch appeared immediately, called the child Rapunzel after the name of the herbs the mother had eaten, and took it away with her.

Rapunzel grew into the most beautiful child under the sun. When she was twelve, the witch shut her up at the top of a high tower which lay deep in the forest and had neither door nor stairs, only a tiny window right at the top. Whenever the witch wanted to enter the tower, she would call up from below, 'Rapunzel, Rapunzel, let down your hair!'

Rapunzel had beautiful long hair, as fine as spun gold. When she heard the witch call her, she would unbraid her hair, make it fast round the window latch, and then let it tumble down to the witch, who would climb up to her.

The years passed by, until one day the king's son came riding through the wood near the tower. As he rode he heard the most beautiful singing. He stopped and listened, enchanted. It was Rapunzel, who was whiling away her lonely hours by singing in her sweet, soft voice. The king's son wanted to climb up to her and searched for the door of the tower, but there was none to be found. He rode home, but the singing had so moved his heart that day after day he rode to the wood to listen.

One day, as he stood hidden behind a tree, he saw the witch arrive, and heard her call, 'Rapunzel, Rapunzel, let down your hair!' Rapunzel let down her beautiful long tresses, and the witch climbed up.

'If that is the ladder one must use, then I will try my luck,' murmured the king's son to himself. And the following day at dusk he went to the tower, and called, 'Rapunzel, Rapunzel, let down your hair!' At once the long tresses came rippling down to him, and the king's son began to climb.

At first Rapunzel was frightened when she saw a young man climbing into her room, but the king's son gently explained how her beautiful singing had so entranced him that he could find no peace until he had seen her for himself.

Soon Rapunzel lost her fear, and when the young and handsome king's son asked her to be his wife she thought, 'He will love me better than the old woman.' So she laid her hand in his, and said, 'Yes, I will marry you and go with you gladly, but how am I to climb down the tower? Each time you come here you must bring me a silken cord, and I will make a ladder with it. When it is finished I shall climb down, and you shall take me away on your horse.'

They agreed that he would come every evening until the ladder was ready, for the old woman came by day. The witch knew nothing of what was going on until one day Rapunzel asked her, 'Why are you so much heavier to pull up than the young prince? He is with me in a twinkling.'

'You wicked child!' cried the witch. 'What is this I hear? I thought I had kept you well hidden from the whole world, and yet you have deceived me!'

In her anger she seized Rapunzel's beautiful hair, took her scissors and – snip, snap – cut it off. There on the floor lay the lovely golden tresses. The old witch was so angry and merciless that she carried Rapunzel away to a barren wilderness, and left her there to live in wretchedness and misery.

As dusk was falling that evening, the witch returned from the wilderness to the tower, where she had fastened Rapunzel's long hair to the window latch. When the young prince stood below and called, 'Rapunzel, Rapunzel, let down your hair' – she lowered the hair to him. He climbed up, but when he reached the top he found not his dearest Rapunzel, but the witch, who glared at him with baleful eyes.

'So,' she cried scornfully, 'you have come to find your lady-love! But the cat has taken your sweet little singing-bird from the nest, and is waiting to catch you too! You will never see Rapunzel again. For you she is as good as lost.'

The grief of the king's son was so great that he could not bear it, and in despair he leaped from the window. He escaped with his life, but the thorn bushes in which he landed blinded him. He wandered sightless through the wood, finding only roots and wild berries to eat, lamenting and weeping over the loss of his dear bride.

He roamed the world for some years in great misery,

and eventually came to the wilderness where Rapunzel lived. He heard the dear, familiar voice, and hastened towards it. As he approached, Rapunzel recognized him and fell on his neck, weeping. Two of her tears dropped on to his eyelids. At once his eyes became clear and he could see as perfectly as ever.

He took her back to his kingdom, where he was welcomed with great joy, and they lived happily and contentedly for many, many years.

The Old Woman of the Forest

Once upon a time a poor servant-girl was travelling through a dark forest with her master and mistress and their servants. When they reached the heart of the forest they were attacked by robbers, who leapt from a thicket and killed everyone, except for the servant-girl. She had jumped from the coach in fright and had hidden behind a tree.

After the robbers had left with their booty, the servant-girl came out of hiding. When she saw the dreadful work they had done, she began to weep bitterly. 'What shall I do?' she sobbed. 'I cannot find my way out of this forest alone, and there's not a soul living here. I shall certainly starve to death.'

She looked about for a path, but could find none. When evening came she sat down beneath a tree, determined to go no further, no matter what happened.

After a while a little white dove flew down to her, with a tiny golden key in its beak. It laid the key in her hand, saying, 'Do you see that big tree over there? There is a

little lock in it. Open it with the key, and you will find food inside. You need go hungry no longer.'

The girl went to the tree and unlocked it. Inside she found a little bowl of milk and enough fine white bread to satisfy her hunger. When she could eat no more, she yawned and said, 'I am so tired. If only I had my bed here!'

Down flew the dove once more, with another golden key in its beak 'Open that tree over there,' it said, 'and you will find a bed.' She opened the tree, and found a beautiful, soft bed. She said her prayers, lay down, and was soon fast asleep.

In the morning the dove flew down again with yet another key, saying, 'Open the tree behind you, and you will find clothes.'

And when the girl opened it, she found beautiful garments worked with gold and jewels, more magnificent than those of any king's daughter.

And so she lived in the forest for some time, while the

dove cared for all her daily needs. It was a good and quiet life.

One day, however, the dove asked her, 'Will you do something for me now?'

'Gladly, gladly,' she cried.

'I will take you to a little house in the forest,' said the dove. 'When you go in, you will see an old woman sitting by the fire. She will ask you what you want, but pay no heed, and say nothing. Pass to the right of her, and you will come to a door. Open this, and you will find yourself in a room where all kinds of rings lie on a table, many of them made of gold and set with diamonds, emeralds, rubies, and all sorts of precious stones. Leave them alone, and look for a plain copper ring. Bring that to me as quickly as you can.'

The girl followed the dove to the little house, and went in. There sat an old woman, who stared at her as she entered, and asked, 'What are you looking for, child?' The girl said nothing, and crossed the room to the little door. 'Where are you going?' shrieked the old woman, seizing her skirt and trying to pull her back. 'This is my house, and no one can come in unless I say so.'

Not a word did the girl speak. She tugged herself free and went straight into the little room. There, glittering and gleaming on the table, lay hundreds and hundreds of rings. She rummaged quickly through them, looking for the plain copper ring, but she could not find it. While she was still searching, she suddenly noticed the old woman trying to slip from the room, a birdcage in her hand.

She ran to the old woman and snatched the cage from her. And when she looked inside, she saw a bird with the plain copper ring in its beak. The girl took the ring and ran happily out of the house, thinking that the white dove would come to take the ring. But it did not come, and so she leant against a tree to wait. As she stood there, the tree seemed to move behind her, and lowered its branches. They suddenly twined themselves about her – and became two arms. When she looked round she saw that the tree was a handsome man, who kissed her and said, 'You have saved me and set me free from the power of the old woman, who is a wicked witch. She turned me into a tree, and allowed me to fly about as a white dove only for an hour or so every day. As long as she possessed the ring, I could not win back my human form.'

All round them stood his servants and horses, who had also been turned into trees and had been freed with their master. So the young man took the servant-girl back with him to his kingdom – for he was a king's son – and there they were married, and lived happily ever after.

Oda and the Snake

There was once a man who had three daughters, and the youngest was called Oda. One day he was going into the town to market, and he asked his daughters what they would like. 'I should like a golden spinning-wheel,' said the eldest. 'I should like a golden harp,' said the second. But Oda said, 'Just bring me whatever crosses your path on the way home.'

So the man rode into the town, did his business there, and bought the presents the two elder daughters had asked for. Then he set off for home.

When he had travelled some distance, he stopped for a

rest. He saw a snake glide beneath his cart, and remembering Oda's request, he caught the creature and threw it into the back of the cart. When he arrived home, he took the snake, laid it gently on the doorstep, and left it lying there.

As soon as Oda came to the door, the snake began to speak. 'Oda, dear Oda, take me into the hall!'

'What!' exclaimed Oda. 'My father has already brought you as far as the door, and now you want to be allowed into the hall!' Nevertheless, she did as it asked, and took the snake into the hall.

Oda was about to go to her room, when the snake called after her, 'Oda, dear Oda, let me lie at your doorway!'

'My goodness!' she said. 'My father brought you to our house, and I carried you into the hall, and now you want to lie at my bedroom door!' Nevertheless, she did as it asked, and set it gently down at her door.

As Oda made to go into her room the snake called out once again. 'Oda, dear Oda, let me come in and lie beside your bed!'

'Whoever heard of such a thing!' exclaimed Oda crossly. 'My father brought you to our house, I carried you into the hall and set you down at my bedroom door, and now you want to come right into my bedroom! Oh, very well! If it will satisfy you, come in!'

So she laid the snake down beside her bed; but as she jumped into bed, she heard the snake's voice yet again. 'Oda, dear Oda, let me lie on the bed, where it is warm and soft.'

'This is too much!' cried Oda in vexation. 'My father brought you to our house, I carried you into the hall and set you down at my door, and even brought you in beside my bed, and now you want to lie on the bed! Are you cold, or what is the matter? Oh, very well then. But you must lie still!'

So she lifted up the cold snake in her kind hands and laid it on the soft, warm coverlet. All at once the snake became a handsome young prince, who had been bewitched for many years and who had now been set free by Oda's kindness.

The prince took Oda to be his wife and so she became a queen.

Jorinda and Joringel

Once upon a time there was a castle in the heart of a deep, thick forest. In the castle, all alone, there lived an old, old woman, who was a powerful witch. By day she turned herself into a cat or a screech-owl, but by night she took on her human form. If any man came within a hundred yards of her castle he was immediately turned to stone, and could not move unless she set him free. But if a young girl came within the magic circle the old witch would turn her into a bird, put her in a bird-basket, and carry the basket to a room in the castle, where she had more than seven thousand baskets of such rare birds.

Now there was a young girl called Jorinda, as beautiful as the day, and she was to be married to a handsome young man called Joringel. The day of their wedding was not far off, and one evening they wandered deep into the forest to be alone and to talk together.

It was a fine evening. The sun shone brightly between the trees into the deep green of the wood, and the turtledoves cooed softly in the beeches. The young couple wandered happily for some time, but when at last they looked about to find the way home they realized that they were lost. They sat down beneath the trees to think what they could do.

The sun was just beginning to set when Joringel glimpsed the grey walls of the castle through the trees. A cold shudder ran through him, and he was filled with fear. Jorinda was softly singing.

'My little bird with scarlet wing
Sang sorrow, sorrow, sorrow!
He to the dove his grief did sing,
Sing sorrow, sorrow, so—soocoo, soocoo, soocoo!'

Joringel looked round in alarm, and saw that Jorinda had become a nightingale warbling. 'Soocoo, soocoo, soocoo.' A screech-owl with fiery eyes flew three times round them, and three times cried, 'Shu-hu-hu-hu.' Joringel found he could neither move nor speak, for he had been turned to stone.

By now the sun had set. The owl flew into a thicket, and immediately there emerged a scrawny, bent old woman. She had red eyes and a long hooked nose which almost touched her chin. Muttering to herself, she caught the nightingale and carried it away on her hand.

At length the old woman returned, and said to Joringel, 'Greetings, my friend. When the first rays of moonlight strike you, you will be free.' Just then the moon rose above the trees, and Joringel threw himself on his knees in front of the old woman, begging her to bring Jorinda back to him.

'You shall never have her back!' she screeched. 'You will never see her again!'

Broken-hearted, Joringel turned to go, and came at length to a village where no one knew him. For many months he worked there as a shepherd, and often he would wander back to the castle where Jorinda was imprisoned.

One night he dreamed that he found a blood-red flower, in the heart of which lay a large and beautiful pearl. He plucked the flower and took it to the castle, and everything he touched with it was freed from enchantment.

When he awoke in the morning, he set out to search through the mountains and glens for the magical blood-red flower. At last he found it, just as the ninth day was dawning. A dew-drop glistened in the heart of the flower, as big as the most beautiful pearl.

He picked the flower, and journeyed through the day and night until he came to the castle. He went straight to the great doors and touched them with the flower. They sprang open at once, and he went in. He crossed the courtyard, and followed the sound of birds to an enormous room where he found the witch feeding her seven thousand captive birds. When she saw Joringel, she cursed and spat poison at him, but she was unable to touch him. He paid her no heed, and began to examine the bird-baskets.

There were hundreds of nightingales! How was he to tell which was his Jorinda? As he stood perplexed he saw the old woman creeping away with a bird-basket in her hand. Quick as a flash he leapt after her and touched the basket and the old woman with the red flower. At its touch the witch lost all her power, and Jorinda stood before Joringel, as beautiful as ever. Joringel changed all the other birds back into young girls, and then returned home with his Jorinda. And they lived contentedly together for the rest of their lives.

Half of Everything

A merchant had three sons. When they grew up, their father said to them, 'I want to see what sort of merchants you will make. Here are one hundred guilders each. Go into the town and buy your wares.'

The two elder brothers went together, leaving the youngest on his own, for they considered him a simpleton, who would only cause embarrassment. They each bought as much as they could with their hundred guilders, and when they returned home their father praised them and was well pleased.

The youngest son also set out for town, but on the way he saw a man lying dead by the road. He ran at once to the nearest village to ask why the man had been left lying there. 'There is no one to pay for the funeral,' the people said.

'I will pay for it,' said the simpleton, and gave fifty guilders for a decent funeral. Satisfied, he hurried on to the big town, where he bought goods with his remaining fifty guilders.

When he reached home he told his father what he had done. The old man was angry with him for wasting money. 'If you do not look after your money better next time, you will have to leave my house!'

Not long afterwards the man again sent his three sons into the town, and this time he gave them each two hundred guilders to spend. The two elder brothers spent their money wisely, and their father was pleased with them.

But on his way through the town the youngest son saw

a beautiful young girl standing at a barred prison window. He stopped to ask what she had done, and she told him tearfully that she had been wrongly accused of stealing a hundred guilders.

The young fellow felt so sorry for her that he went to the court. 'The girl is innocent,' he said. 'Set her free, and I will pay the hundred guilders until the real thief is caught.'

So they set her free. But the young girl was the king's daughter, who visited the poor every day in disguise. By chance, she had been in the streets when the money was stolen, and had been dragged off to prison. In gratitude for what he had done she gave the young fellow a gold ring, saying, 'This will help me to recognize you again!'

The young man bought goods with his remaining hundred guilders, and returned home, satisfied. He told his father about the girl he had rescued from prison, but the old man was angry. 'You have no sense at all,' he said. 'Away with you – out of my sight!'

So the young man had to leave home with only a few guilders in his pocket. As he sat by the roadside one day, wondering what to do, an old man in a grey cloak came by and asked why he was so unhappy. So the young man told his sad story.

The old man comforted him. 'If you will promise to give me half of all you possess at the end of seven years, I will tell you how to find your fortune.'

'I'll promise that gladly,' said the young fellow.

'Hurry into the city then,' said the old man, 'and you will find the king's daughter waiting for you!' So saying, he went on his way, and the young man set off for the city.

A great many nobles and princes had already come to the king's court to woo the princess, but so far she had rejected them all. But, as soon as the young man arrived, the king's daughter saw the ring on his finger and cried, 'This is the one!' Joyfully she led him to her father, the king, who gave them his blessing. They were married soon after, and in due course the young man became king of the land.

At the end of seven happy and peaceful years the old man in the grey cloak suddenly appeared and demanded half of all the young king's possessions, as he had been promised. True to his word, the king divided all he had and gave the old man half. But the bargain was not yet complete: the old man demanded half of his wife, the queen.

'But how am I to do that?' asked the king in dismay.

'Quite simple,' answered the old man. 'Cut her in two.'

The young king was horror-struck, but he thought for a while and then said, 'I love her too much to harm a hair of her head. But I do not want to break my promise. Take all of her.'

'Keep everything!' cried the old man. 'You have kept your promise to me!' And he vanished before the young king's eyes.

The Wishing-ring

A young farmer, whose work was going badly, sat resting on his plough, wiping the sweat from his brow. All at once an old witch crept up to him and said, 'Why are you wasting time worrying? Just follow your nose for two whole days until you come to a great pine tree that stands on its own, towering above all the other trees of the forest. If you can fell it, your fortune is made.'

The farmer did not need to be told twice, but took his axe and set out. At the end of two days he came to the pine tree and set to work with his axe without delay. As the huge tree came crashing to the ground, a bird's nest with two eggs in it fell out of the topmost branches. The eggs rolled on to the ground and were broken; and out of one egg crawled a baby eagle, while from the other fell a little gold ring. The eagle at once began to grow, until he was half the size of a full-grown man. He flapped his wings, and cried, 'You have set me free. As a reward, you may take the gold ring. It is a wishing-ring. If you turn it on your finger and at the same time make a wish, the wish will immediately be fulfilled. But there is only one wish in the ring. Once it has been made, the ring will lose its power, and be like any ordinary ring. Consider well what you will wish, so that you have no cause for regret.'

With these words the eagle rose into the air, and for some time swooped above the farmer's head; then it shot like an arrow towards the sun, until it disappeared from sight.

The farmer put the ring on his finger, and set off for home. As evening fell he came to a town. There stood a goldsmith with many fine rings for sale. The farmer showed the goldsmith his ring, and asked him how much it was worth. 'A mere trifle,' said the goldsmith. The farmer laughed, and explained that it was a wishing-ring, worth far more than all the rings the goldsmith had for sale.

Now the goldsmith was a dishonest, cunning fellow. He asked the farmer to spend the night with him as his guest.

But as the farmer slept the goldsmith secretly removed the wishing-ring from his finger, replacing it with an ordinary gold ring.

Early next morning the goldsmith could hardly wait to turn the farmer out of the house. He woke him at the crack of dawn, and said, 'You have a long journey ahead of you, my friend. I think you should be on your way.'

As soon as the farmer had left, the goldsmith hurried to his room and closed the shutters so that no one could see him. He bolted the door behind him, turned the ring on his finger, and said, 'I want a million gold sovereigns immediately.'

Hardly had the words left his mouth than it began to rain gold sovereigns – hard, shiny sovereigns, which fell heavily over his head, shoulders, and arms. He cried out with pain and leapt for the door, but before he could reach it to undo the bolts he fell to the floor, cut and bleeding. The shower of sovereigns fell steadily and showed no sign of stopping. The weight of the coins soon broke the floor, and the goldsmith went crashing with his gold into the cellar below. The rain of gold continued until the million sovereigns were complete and the goldsmith lay dead in his cellar, buried beneath a mountain of gold.

Meanwhile the farmer reached home and showed his ring to his wife. 'Now we cannot fail to make our fortune,' he said. 'We must think very carefully how we shall use our wish.'

But his wife knew at once what to wish for. 'What do you think of wishing for more land? We have so little, and the wedge of land that separates our two fields makes life very difficult for us.'

'Certainly it would be well worth having that land,' replied the farmer. 'Perhaps we could earn enough money to buy it, if we worked very hard for a year.' So for a whole year the man and his wife both worked hard in the fields, and the harvest was so good that they earned enough to buy the wedge of land, and still had some money left over. 'This is grand!' exclaimed the man. 'We have our land, and some money to spare, and we have not used up our wish yet.'

Then his wife thought it would be a good idea to wish for a cow and a horse. 'Let's not fritter away our wish like that,' said the farmer, clinking the spare money in his pocket. 'It will not take us long to earn enough to buy a horse and cow.'

Sure enough, in less than a year they had earned enough money to buy a fine strong horse and a beautiful cow. 'How lucky we are,' said the man. 'We have not used our wish, and yet we have everything we want!'

But the woman still wanted him to use the wish, and said to him at last, 'What has happened to you? I hardly know you nowadays. You used to complain at the slightest thing and feel so sorry for yourself. But now, when you can wish for the whole world, you work and slave and seem quite contented with your lot. You could be a king if you wanted, or the wealthiest farmer in the whole world, with coffers full of gold – yet you cannot make up your mind what to choose.'

'Stop pestering and nagging,' said the farmer. 'We are both still young and we have all our life before us. The ring has only one wish, and that will be quickly used up. Who knows when we shall be in difficulties and shall want to use the ring? Do we need anything? Haven't we been so successful since we have had the ring that we are the envy of all our neighbours? In the meantime, be content with thinking what to wish for.'

With that the matter was at an end for the time being, and it really seemed as if the ring had brought luck to the house and the farm, for the barns and store-rooms were full to overflowing. Year followed year, and the poor, thin farmer became a rich, fat farmer, who worked hard in the fields with his men as if he meant to earn the whole world. But on summer evenings he sat at his front door, comfortable and contented with life, nodding a good evening to all who passed.

So the years went by. Now and then, when they were alone and there was no one by to hear, the woman would remind her husband of the ring and make all kinds of suggestions for wishes. But the farmer would reply that they still had time. And so his wife reminded him less and less often, until the ring was scarcely ever mentioned. From time to time the farmer would still twiddle the ring on his finger and look at it, but he was always very careful not to make a wish.

After thirty or forty years the farmer and his wife had grown old and their hair was snowy-white, and they had still not used up their wish. And then, both on the same night, they died peacefully in their sleep.

At the funeral their children and their children's children stood sadly round the two coffins. One of them wanted to take off his father's ring, but the eldest son said, 'No, let Father take his ring into the grave with him. When he was alive he had his own little mystery about it, and I often caught Mother looking at it. It must be a keepsake – Mother probably gave it to him when they were young.'

So the ring was buried with the old farmer – a wishing-ring which was not really a wishing-ring, but which had nevertheless brought as much good fortune to the house as any man could have wished for. For a poor thing in the hands of a good man is always worth much more than a good thing in the hands of a bad man.

Simeli Hill

There were once two brothers, of whom one was rich and the other poor. The rich brother gave nothing to his poor brother, who often could not afford to buy bread for his wife and children.

One day the poor brother was pushing his hand-cart through the woods, when he came upon a rocky hillock which he had never seen before. He gazed at it, open-mouthed, but not for long. Twelve wild-looking men came marching through the woods. He thought they must be robbers, so he quickly hid his cart and climbed a tree, where he waited to see what would happen.

The twelve men went straight past his tree and stopped at the foot of the hillock. 'Semsi Hill, Semsi Hill, open up!' they cried.

A wide split appeared in the rocky hillock, and the twelve men trooped in, the split closing up behind them. After a while it opened again and the men came out with heavy sacks on their shoulders. The last man out turned and said, 'Semsi Hill, Semsi Hill, close up!' – and the split closed, leaving no sign to show where it had been.

When the twelve men were out of sight, the poor man climbed down from his tree, curious to know what was hidden in the hillock. 'Semsi Hill, Semsi Hill, open up!' he said. The hillside opened, and in he went. He found himself in a vast cave full of gold and silver, and countless heaps of pearls and glittering jewels.

The poor fellow stood gazing in amazement at the treasure, wondering whether he should take anything. At last he filled his pockets with gold, but he did not touch the pearls or the precious stones. When he came out of the hillock he turned and said, 'Semsi Hill, Semsi Hill, close up!' The split in the hillside closed, and the poor man returned home.

Now all his troubles were over. He lived well and happily, gave generously to the poor and did good to everybody. When the money came to an end, however, he went to his rich brother and borrowed a bucket, which he used to fetch more gold from the hillock; but still he left the jewels untouched. When the time came for a third visit, he again borrowed his brother's bucket. But the rich

brother had been jealous for a long time and could not understand where all this wealth was coming from – nor what his brother wanted with his bucket. He was a cunning fellow, and he poured tar into the bottom of the bucket. When the bucket was returned to him he found a gold coin stuck in the tar, so he went to his brother and asked, 'What have you been measuring in my bucket?'

'Corn and barley,' came the reply.

Then the rich brother showed him the gold piece in the tar, and threatened to bring him to trial if he did not tell the truth. So the poor brother told him all about Semsi Hill and its treasure.

Without wasting a moment the rich brother took his

horse and cart and drove to the hillock. 'Semsi Hill, Semsi Hill, open up!' he cried. The split opened up, and so many treasures lay spread before him that he did not know where to begin. At last he decided on the jewels, and filled his sacks to the brim. But he had been so absorbed in the treasure that he had completely forgotten the name of the hill by the time he wanted to leave. 'Simeli Hill, Simeli Hill, open up!' he cried. But the hillside remained firmly closed. The rich brother grew frightened, but the more he tried to remember the more confused he became.

In the evening the hillock opened, and the twelve wild-looking men trooped in. They laughed loudly when they saw the intruder, and shouted, 'Caught at last, magpie! This time you shan't escape!'

'It wasn't me,' the rich brother cried in fear. 'It was my brother!' But, though he begged and pleaded, the twelve men would not listen, and he was shut in a dark cavern in the depths of the hill.

The Haunted Room

A grocer had gone to town and wanted to find a night's lodging at an inn which he visited from time to time, but every bed was taken and all the corridors and rooms were swarming like a beehive. The innkeeper was most put out, for the grocer was a good customer, and he hated having to refuse him a bed.

'We are so full up tonight,' said the innkeeper, 'that I simply do not know where to put you. There is only one room free, but that is haunted, and I should not like to put you there.'

'Haunted, is it?' exclaimed the grocer. 'As long as I have a good bed, not even a howling tom-cat can wake me once my head is on the pillow. Give me the room – the ghosts won't bother me.'

The innkeeper was greatly relieved, and as soon as the servant-girl had made up the bed the grocer lay down and fell asleep at once, for he was very tired.

He had been asleep for about two hours when he was awakened by a loud noise at the door. He sat up in bed and looked across the room to see where it was coming from. To his astonishment he saw the door open, although it had been firmly locked and bolted. A little old man with a long,

grey beard came in, crossed the room with a key in his hand, and opened a safe in the wall. He took a razor and soap, a shaving-brush and a towel out of the safe, and laid them all neatly on the table. He prepared a lather, and beckoned to the grocer.

The grocer felt a little uneasy, but he climbed out of bed, pulled on his breeches and went to sit on the chair which the old man offered him. The old man began to lather the grocer's face vigorously, and shaved him so smoothly that there was not a single hair left on his face. When he had finished, he cleaned the razor and the brush and laid them neatly together on the table. He looked sadly at the grocer, and began to leave.

Now the grocer was a polite fellow and had always heard that a kindness should always be repaid by another kindness. So he told the little old man to sit down, tucked the towel round his neck. and began to shave off the long grey beard. And he shaved it so smoothly that there was not a single hair left on the old man's face. Then he laid the brush and razor neatly together on the table, just as the old man had done.

The old man smiled happily, nodded his thanks, and handed the grocer the key to the safe. Then off he went.

When the grocer opened the safe. he found an immense treasure inside. Now he was a wealthy man, and he became the greatest merchant in all the land.

The Little Golden Fish

On a sandy beach beside the sea there was once a tiny little tumbledown shack where an old fisherman lived with his wife. They were very poor, and eked out a meagre existence from the few small fishes which the man caught in his net.

One day the fisherman drew his net in from the sea, but it was so much heavier than usual that he could hardly drag it up the beach. When he looked to see what he had caught, however, there was nothing in the net apart from one tiny fish. But it was no ordinary fish : it was of purest gold.

'Throw me back, dear fisherman,' pleaded the little fish in a human voice. 'Let me swim back into the deep blue sea. I will repay your kindness. I will make all your wishes come true.'

The fisherman was a kind-hearted fellow, so he threw the fish back into the sea, saying, 'You are not worth much to me in any case. Back you go into the sea.'

'What did you catch?' asked his wife when he came in.

'Only one little golden fish – but I threw it back. It pleaded so hard with me, and it even promised to make my wishes come true! I felt sorry for the tiny thing, so I let it go.'

'What a fool you are!' said the woman angrily. 'For the first time in your life you find a treasure in your net – and you let it go! I've no patience with you.' And so the scolding went on from early morning till late at night. The poor fisherman had no peace. 'You might at least have asked the fish for a loaf of bread. We haven't a crumb in the house for supper,' his wife complained bitterly.

At last the old man could stand it no longer. He went down to the shore and called out, 'Little fish, little fish, come here!'

Soon the little golden fish appeared, swishing its tail. 'What do you want, old fellow?' it asked.

'My old wife is angry with me, and has sent me to ask for bread.'

'Go home again,' said the fish. 'You have plenty of bread.'

So he went home, and asked. 'Have we enough bread now, old woman?'

'Oh, we have plenty of bread, but just look at our rain-barrel. It has fallen to pieces. Go back and tell the little fish that we want a new rain-barrel.'

So the old man went to the shore, and called, 'Little fish, little fish, come here!'

The fish came swimming up. 'What do you want, old man?' it asked.

'My old wife has sent me to ask you for a new rain-barrel.'

'All right,' said the fish. 'You shall have a fine new rain-barrel.'

The old man went home, and as soon as he came within sight of his hut he saw a new green rain-barrel beside the door. But his wife was waiting for him, and she sent him straight back to ask the fish for a new hut. 'You cannot expect me to live any longer in this tumbledown old shack!'

Back the fisherman went to the shore, and called, 'Little fish, little fish, come here!'

The fish swam up to him, and asked, 'What do you want, old man?'

'Little fish, please build us a nice new hut. My old wife is always scolding and will not leave me in peace until she has a new hut.'

'Do not worry,' said the fish. 'Go home and you will find your new hut.'

Home the fisherman went, and there in place of his old shack was a new hut built of fine oak timbers, beautifully carved and decorated. The old woman came running to meet him, angrier than ever. 'You old idiot, why can't you make use of your good fortune? Do you think a hut is all I want? I'm tired of living like a slave. I want to be a countess with a retinue of servants.'

Once again the old man ran back to the sea and summoned the fish.

'My old wife has become quite unreasonable. She will not be satisfied until she is a countess, with all sorts of servants.'

'Very well,' said the fish. 'Go home, and you will find your wish fulfilled.'

The old man ran home, to find an immense three-storeyed mansion in the place of his hut. Footmen were hurrying to and fro across the courtyard, and the cook was busy in the kitchen, while the fisherman's wife sat in a long velvet gown, giving out her orders. 'How do you like this, dear wife?' asked the old man.

'You stupid lout!' she shouted. 'How, dare you call me your wife! Hey, footmen! Take away this dirty old fellow, and give him a good beating!'

Instantly a small army of footmen came running up, and took the poor old fisherman away to the stable, where he was sorely beaten, and given nothing but dry crusts to eat. What a miserable life the old fisherman led! Every day he had to sweep the courtyard, and if he left a single grain of dust lying he was hauled away to the stable and beaten.

So it went on for some time, until the woman became bored with being a countess. She ordered the old man to be brought before her. 'Off you go,' she said, 'and tell the fish I want to be an empress.'

The old man stood by the sea, and called softly, 'Little fish, little fish, come here!'

'What do you want, old man?' asked the fish.

'My old wife is more difficult than ever,' he replied. 'Now she will be satisfied with nothing less than being an empress.'

'Don't worry, old man,' said the fish. 'She shall have what she wants.'

So the fisherman ran off home again. He found that the three-storeyed mansion had been replaced by a towering palace with golden domes, before which all the royal troops were drawn up on a wide green meadow. As the old man stood staring, the old woman, dressed in full imperial regalia and accompanied by her generals and field-marshals, appeared on the balcony to review her troops. The trumpets brayed, the drums rolled, and the soldiers cheered.

Before long, however, the old woman was tired of being an empress, so she ordered her generals and field-marshals to bring the old man before her throne. The order caused great confusion and embarrassment. 'Which old man does Her Majesty mean?' they wondered, as they rushed to and fro, looking for him.

After a long and troublesome search they found the old fisherman hidden away in a corner, and led him before the throne. 'Off you go to your goldfish, old donkey,' she ordered. 'Tell him I am tired of being an empress. I want to be Queen of the Sea, ruler of all the fishes and oceans of the whole world.'

The old man would not go at first, but she threatened to have him beheaded if he refused. So off he went, and called, 'Little fish, little fish, come here!' There was no sign of the fish.

The old man called again – but it still did not come. He called a third time. The sea began to swirl and heave, and the sky grew dark and menacing. At last the little golden fish appeared. 'What do you want, old man?'

'My old wife is quite mad,' he replied. 'She now wants to be Queen of the Sea, ruler of all the fishes and oceans of the whole world.'

Not a word did the golden fish utter, but turned about and disappeared into the depths of the ocean. The old man set off home, and as he came up the beach he could hardly believe his eyes Gone was the magnificent palace, as though it had never existed. The tumbledown shack stood in its old place, and inside sat the old woman in her ragged grey skirt.

So life went on as before. Once more the old man went fishing; but though he cast his net as industriously as ever he never again caught the little golden fish.

Master Money and Madam Fortune

Once upon a time Master Money and Madam Fortune fell in love with one another. They were always in each other's company. Like the tail behind a dog, Master Money trailed after Madam Fortune, and people began to say that they would soon be married.

Master Money was stout and thick set, with a round head made of gold from Peru, a body of silver from Mexico, and legs of pure copper. Madam Fortune was a chatterbox, moody and capricious, inconstant, and blind as a mole.

Hardly was the wedding over than they began to quarrel. Madam Fortune wanted everything her own way, but that was not at all to the liking of the proud Master Money. As neither would give way to the other, they decided to have a test to see which of them was the more powerful.

'Look,' said the woman to her husband. 'There is a poor ragged fellow sitting at the foot of the olive tree. Let us see which of us can give him the better life.'

Master Money agreed, and out they went to the olive tree. The man was so poor and unfortunate that he had never set eyes on either of them during his whole life. His eyes popped out of his head like two black olives when he caught sight of the distinguished couple approaching him.

'God bless you,' said Master Money.

'And Your Excellency likewise,' replied the poor man.

'Do you not recognize me?'

'No, Your Honour, but here I am at your service,' said the man.

'Have you never set eyes on me before?'

'No, never.'

'Then you have no possessions?'

'Oh yes, sir. I have six children, naked as onions and with rags for shoes. But as for anything else, it has always been a case of "Wait and see"'

'Why are you not working?'

'Because I cannot find a job. I have such bad luck that everything I start goes wrong. A man employed me to dig a well for him here, and promised me a handsome reward if I struck water. But he would pay nothing in advance.'

'Sensible fellow!' exclaimed Master Money. 'But continue.'

'I worked extremely hard, until the sweat was pouring off my back – for I am not as weak as I look.'

'I can well believe that,' said Master Money.

'I dug and dug, deeper and deeper, day after day, but not a drop of water did I find. It seemed as if the centre of the earth had dried up.'

'I will help you, my friend,' said Master Money, handing the poor man a coin. The poor fellow at first thought he was dreaming, but then he took the coin and ran like a greyhound straight to the baker's to buy bread. However, when he put his hand in his pocket to take out the coin he found nothing but the hole through which the coin had made its escape. In despair he crawled about by the road-side, scrabbling in the dust in the hope of finding his lost coin. But how could he possibly know where to look? With the coin he lost time, and with time he lost his temper, and he began to curse his bad luck.

Madam Fortune nearly split her sides laughing, and Master Money's face became yellower than ever with rage.

There was nothing for it but to delve once more into his money-bag and give the poor man more coins.

The poor man was wild with joy, and this time, instead of going to the baker's, he went to the draper's to buy some clothes for his wife and children. But when he handed the coins across the counter the draper declared that they were not real and that the poor man must be a forger, who should be brought to justice. The poor fellow was so ashamed at this that you could have made toast on his burning cheeks.

He turned tail and fled straight back to Master Money. When he related his sad experience Madam Fortune was most amused, but Master Money was furious.

'Take this,' he said, giving the poor fellow a handful of gold. 'You have been most unfortunate, but I will help you if it's the last thing I do.'

Quite beside himself and mad with delight the poor man rushed away, only to run into a pair of thieves, who knocked him down and stripped him, and robbed him of his gold.

'Now it is my turn,' said Madam Fortune, with a supercilious smile at her enraged husband. 'We shall soon see which of us has the greater power.' She went up to the poor man, who had thrown himself on the ground and was tearing his hair. She breathed on him gently, and almost immediately he found under his hand the coin he had lost through the hole in his pocket.

'Oh, well,' he sighed. 'Something is better than nothing. I must buy some bread for my poor children. They have had nothing to eat for three days, and their tummies are as empty as hollow nutshells.'

As he passed by the draper's shop the draper called him and apologized for what he had said. He had thought the coins were false, but the goldsmith had called in and had declared that they were genuine. In fact they were probably worth more than ordinary coins of the same sort. He returned the coins, and to make amends he gave the poor man all the clothes he had previously wanted to buy. The poor man accepted the apology and took the clothes under his arm.

As he was crossing the market-place he met the two thieves who had robbed him being taken to prison. The judge, who was the most just judge that ever was, gave back the handful of gold coins to the poor man without charging him anything.

The poor man invested his money in a mine which was being sunk by one of his friends, and they had barely dug five feet below the surface when they found first a vein of gold, then a vein of tin, and finally a vein of iron. Before long the poor man was an exceedingly wealthy man, the envy of all who knew him.

From that time on, Madam Fortune had her husband completely in the hollow of her hand. She is more moody and capricious than ever, and distributes her favours without rhyme or reason. It is even possible that she will turn her attention on you some day.

The Fox and the Cat

The cat one day met Mr Fox in the woods. Mr Fox was a clever, worldly-wise and much respected person, so the cat greeted him warmly.

'Good day to you, Mr Fox. How are you managing in these difficult times?'

The fox looked haughtily down his long nose for a few moments. 'You poor miserable creature,' he said at last. 'You wretched hunter of mice, you shabby good-for-nothing, have you gone quite mad? *You* presume to ask *me* how I am managing? What can *you* do, pray? How many special skills do you have?'

'I have only one skill,' answered the cat modestly.

'And what is that?' asked the fox.

'I can jump up a tree when the dogs are after me, and so escape from their clutches.'

'Is that all!' exclaimed the fox. 'Then I am very sorry for you. I am master of a thousand skills, and I have a whole bag of tricks besides. Come along with me and I will show you how to escape from the dogs.'

Just then a huntsman came into the woods with four hounds. The cat jumped up a tree and climbed quickly to the highest branches, where she hid herself among the leaves.

'Open up your bag of tricks, Mr Fox! Open it up quickly!' she called down. But the hounds had already seized the fox and were holding him fast.

'Oh, Mr Fox!' called the cat. 'Where are your thousand skills and your bagful of tricks now? If you had been able to climb as I can you would have saved your life!'

Little Mary

There was once a woman called Little Mary. She began to weep one day, saying, 'Lord Jesus, if only I had a little milk-cow I should be the happiest person in the whole world! I should be so fond of my cow, and I would look after it well!'

Just then the Lord Jesus came by, and said to her, 'Go home, little Mary. Go home and you will find what you want.'

Little Mary ran home and found a beautiful spotted cow. Next day the Lord Jesus passed by once more, and asked, 'Well, little Mary? Are you satisfied?'

'Yes, Lord, but . . . but . . .'

'But? But what?'

'Nothing, Lord, but . . . you see . . . if only I had a little cottage, how happy I should be.'

'Very well, little Mary,' said the Lord. 'There you are.' And he gave her the cottage, and asked her again next day if she were satisfied.

'Yes, Lord,' she replied. 'But . . . but . . .'

'But? But what?'

'Nothing . . . only that all my neighbours are so beautifully dressed. If I had a new dress, everything would be perfect. How well I should be able to dance in my new dress!'

'Go home, little Mary. You will find what you want there.'

Mary was very pleased with the dress. Next day the Lord asked her again if she were satisfied.

'Yes, Lord,' she said. 'But . . . but . . .'

'Another but! Will you never have enough?'

'If only I had a few hens that would lay dozens of eggs, and . . .'

'Go home, little Mary. You will find what you want there.'

Little Mary found a flock of hens, which were a delight to see. But next day when the Lord asked her, 'Are you satisfied now, little Mary?' – she again replied, 'Yes, Lord. But . . . but . . .'

'But? Another but! Are you not contented yet!'

'Well, you see, Lord,' said Little Mary, 'I have a lovely cow, a new cottage, a beautiful dress, and a fine flock of hens . . . but I am so lonely! I want to get married.'

'Very well. I will arrange for you to meet a good young man who will marry you.'

And very soon Little Mary married the mayor of the town. Shortly after the wedding the Lord came along and asked, 'Well, little Mary, are you happy at last?'

'I? Happy? I am no longer Little Mary with the spotted cow. Do you not know that I am the Lady Mary, wife of the mayor of this town!'

Who Can Tell the Bigger Lie?

One day a nobleman was driving in his carriage, which was drawn by two remarkably thin horses. As he drove along he saw a farmer ploughing a field, and the plough was drawn by two strong, well-built horses.

'Will you change horses with me?' the nobleman asked the farmer. 'Your horses would look better in front of my carriage, and my horses would be more suitable for your plough.'

'That may well be,' said the farmer, 'but I prefer to keep my own horses.'

The nobleman would not give up and pestered the farmer so much that at last it was agreed that all four horses should belong to whoever could tell the bigger lie.

The nobleman had no doubt that he would win, for he was an accomplished liar. The farmer allowed him the honour of beginning, and the nobleman told the following lie. 'My father had seven herds of mares, which gave so much milk that he could drive seven mills with it and grind all the corn in the entire country.'

'That is quite possible,' said the farmer. 'My father had so many beehives that he would not have had time to count them all if he had lived to be five hundred. One day one of the bees did not return to its hive at night. My father noticed its absence at once, and sent me off to look for it, saying that I was not to return home till I had found it.

'I travelled through every country in the whole world, but I could not find the missing bee anywhere. I climbed up to Heaven and searched in every cloud, but she was not there. So then I thought she could only be in Hell. Down I went — but with no success. The bee was nowhere to be found.

'I set off for home feeling very downcast. As I was passing through a forest what should I see but my bee helping an ox to haul a heavy cartload of wood. The other ox had been devoured by a wolf, and the owner of the cart had harnessed my bee in its place.

' "Aha, my friend!" I cried at once. "Do you realize that that is my bee? Unharness it this instant!"

'The man obeyed without hesitation, pleased that I was not angrier. But the harness had hurt my bee's back. I rubbed a little fresh earth into the wound, and it soon healed.

'My father was, of course, delighted when I brought back the missing bee. I told him all about my travels in Heaven and Hell. "And do you know," I said, "that in Heaven I found a long, long table with hundreds of farmers sitting at it, drinking wine, while all I saw in Hell was hundreds of noblemen being roasted on spits!" '

At this the nobleman could contain himself no longer. He leapt to his feet, shouting, 'It's a lie! It's a lie!'

'Yes, my friend,' said the farmer. 'Indeed it is, and I have won the contest!' And the farmer took the nobleman's pair of horses, leaving the proud lord to draw his own carriage home.

Old Sultan

A farmer had a faithful dog, called Sultan. He was old and had lost all his teeth, so that he was no longer of much use on the farm. One evening the farmer said to his wife, 'Tomorrow I shall have to shoot Sultan. We cannot use him any more.'

His wife was sorry for the faithful creature, and said, 'Surely we can afford to feed him in his old age? He has served us well and faithfully for so many years!'

'Don't be soft-hearted!' said the farmer. 'If he has served us well, he has been well fed for it. Now he can no longer work, and no thief would be frightened of him.'

The poor old dog had heard all this, as he lay stretched out in the sun near by, and he was sad to think that the next day would be his last. He was good friends with a shaggy wolf who lived not far away in the forest, and that evening he crept away and poured out all his troubles to him.

'Don't worry, old friend,' said the wolf. 'I know a way to help you. I have an idea. Tomorrow morning go with your master and mistress into the hayfield. They always take their little baby with them and leave him to sleep under the hedge. Lie down as if you are keeping watch, and I will come out of the forest and seize the child, and carry him away. You must chase me, and when I let the child go you must take him back to his parents. They will think you have rescued it, and will be so grateful to you that you will have nothing more to fear. On the contrary, you will have all you want for the rest of your life.'

This seemed an excellent proposal, so the following morning the plan was carried out. The farmer yelled when he saw the wolf running across the field with his baby, and stroked and patted Sultan when he brought the baby back again, safe and sound. 'Not a hair of your head shall be touched,' he said. 'You can stay with us as long as you live, and you will be well looked after.' To his wife he said, 'Go and cook a broth for Sultan which will be easy for him to eat. And give him my pillow for his basket. He has earned it.'

From now on Sultan had nothing to complain of, and soon after he visited his friend the wolf, who was delighted that everything had gone according to plan. 'But, my friend,' said the wolf, 'you will, I hope, turn a blind eye if I steal a fat sheep from time to time. Times are hard, and I often have to go hungry.'

'No,' said Sultan. 'I must be faithful to my master. I cannot allow that!'

The wolf did not really believe that Sultan meant what he said, and that same night he came slinking to the sheep-fold in the dark. The farmer had been warned by the faithful Sultan, and beat the wolf so severely that he turned tail and fled as soon as he could escape, crying, 'Just you wait, you miserable hound! You'll pay for this!'

Next morning the wolf sent the wild boar to bring Sultan out into the forest where they would settle their quarrel. Poor Sultan could find nobody to go with him except an old cat, who had only three legs. As they went along, the old cat limped heavily and stuck her tail straight up in the air because it hurt so much.

The wolf and the wild boar were waiting for them, but when they saw their opponents coming they thought that the cat's tail was a sword, and every time they saw her limp they thought she was picking up a stone to throw at them. They both took fright. and the wild boar crept away to hide in some bushes, while the wolf leapt up a tree for safety.

Sultan and the cat could not understand why there was nobody there, until, suddenly, the cat saw the wild boar's tail sticking out of some bushes. Thinking it was a mouse, she sprang at it and bit it so hard that the boar jumped in the air with a loud snort, and took to his heels, shouting, 'Look up in the tree – there is the one you want!'

Sultan and the cat looked up and saw the wolf crouching on a branch. He was so ashamed of himself that he made peace with the dog, and gave no further trouble.

The Tailor and the Treasure

A tailor, who liked to dress up in silk and velvet and have a merry time, was once invited to a christening. At midnight, when he was on his way home, he wandered from the track and lost his way, for he was tired and had not been looking where he was going.

Before long he realized that he was hemmed in on both sides by trees and behind by thorns and thick undergrowth, while in front of him rose a sheer cliff, split by a narrow cleft just wide enough for a man.

Aha! thought the tailor, here is an adventure! He groped his way into the cleft and looked round for a level spot where he could lie down to sleep. As he fumbled in the darkness, an animal brushed against his ankles, making him stumble. He fell against a heavy iron gate, which creaked open under his weight.

What splendour presented itself to the tailor's eyes! He stood gaping at what he saw: a room, brilliantly lit – but not with lamps or candles. No. The gold and silver of the walls, inlaid with countless jewels, turned the darkness into brightest day. Ranged on each side stood precious caskets, and in the centre of the room an open chest overflowed with glittering gold coins.

A beautiful girl came in through a door in one of the walls and bade him welcome. He would have returned her greeting with a kiss, but she waved him away, saying, 'I have expected you for a long, long time. I have collected all these treasures for you, but they are yours only on one condition: you must kiss me three times, without the slightest hesitation.'

'That would give me great pleasure!' exclaimed the tailor. He was just about to give the first kiss when suddenly the girl changed into a terrible crocodile, and if he had not been taken so much by surprise he might well have hesitated. As it was, he kissed the brute almost involuntarily, and immediately began to tremble all over.

In a flash, the girl was standing before him again, and she looked so lovely that the tailor was already moving forward for the second kiss, when she suddenly turned into a disgusting, fat toad. This shook the tailor to the core, but he gave the toad a hearty kiss on the mouth. Once again the beautiful girl stood before him, smiling so sweetly that he prepared to give the third kiss even more boldly than before.

But, horror! This time the tailor shivered and shook from head to toe, for he was suddenly faced by a long-haired, black billy-goat, bleating and goggling at him. Overcome with panic and disgust he turned and fled from the cave as fast as his legs would carry him. Overhead there was a violent crack of thunder, and a whirlwind buffeted him along so that he could neither hear nor see and at last fell senseless to the ground at the foot of the cliffs.

When he came to there was no trace of the cleft, and he limped sadly away. Since that day, he could not hear of a billy-goat without turning deathly pale and shaking at the knees.

The Farmer and the Devil

There was once a clever farmer, who had spent the day working hard in the fields. The sun was beginning to set and he was thinking of going home when he became aware of a heap of glowing coals not far from where he stood. Puzzled and curious, he went nearer, and saw a little black devil sitting on top of the heap.

'Are you keeping guard over a buried treasure?' asked the farmer.

'Indeed I am,' replied the devil. 'A treasure of more gold and silver than you have seen in your whole life.'

'But the treasure is in my field, and therefore it belongs to me.'

'Yes,' answered the devil. 'It shall be yours if you promise to give me half of everything that grows on your land for two years. I have no shortage of gold and silver, but I have great need of the fruits of the earth.'

The farmer accepted this proposal, saying, 'To avoid any misunderstandings let us agree that whatever grows above the ground shall be yours, and everything below the ground shall be mine.'

This suited the devil very well. But the cunning farmer sowed only turnips that year, and when the devil came to take his share in the autumn he found only withered yellow leaves, while the farmer dug out a fine harvest of turnips.

'All right,' snorted the devil. 'You have made a fool of me this time, but it shall not happen again. Next year *I* will take everything below the ground, and your share shall be whatever grows above the ground.'

'That's only fair,' said the farmer, and when spring came he sowed not turnips, but oats. When the oats were golden and ready to be harvested, the farmer set about reaping, and by the time the devil arrived to claim his share, there was only the stubble left. He was furious at the trick which had been played on him, and he vanished into the earth in a flurry of flames and sparks, while the farmer took a spade and dug up his treasure.

The Little Donkey

There once lived a king and queen who were rich and had everything they wanted, except for a child. The poor queen lamented day and night, saying, 'If only I had a little child!'

At last their wish was fulfilled, but when the baby was born it looked like a baby donkey − not like a human baby at all! The queen was heartbroken when she set eyes on it, and cried, 'I would rather have had no child at all than a donkey! Take it away and throw it into the river!'

'No,' said the king. 'He is God's gift to us, and shall be my son and heir.'

So the little donkey was well cared for, and as the years went by he grew in stature and flaunted a pair of long, straight ears. He was a merry little fellow, always leaping about and playing. His greatest pleasure lay in music, and when he grew older he went to a famous musician and asked, 'Will you teach me to play the lute as well as you?'

'I'm afraid that will be difficult, young sir,' replied the musician. 'Your fingers are hardly suited for playing the lute.'

But the little donkey insisted. He was determined that he would learn to play the lute. and he worked so hard and practised so carefully that he could soon play as well as his teacher.

One day the young prince went for a walk, and came to a spring. He looked in, and saw his donkey reflection in the mirror-clear water. It so upset him that he ran away from home and went out into the wide world.

Over hill and dale travelled the little donkey prince, until he came to a country ruled by an elderly king who had a most lovely daughter. 'I will settle here,' said the little donkey to himself, and he knocked at the palace door, crying, 'Here is a visitor for you. Open up!' The door remained obstinately shut, so he sat down on his haunches, took up his lute and began to play a melody with his front hooves.

The door-keeper stared in astonishment, and then ran to the king. 'There is a little donkey at the door, playing the lute as beautifully as any skilled musician!' he gasped.

'Show this music-maker up to me,' said the king.

When the donkey entered, all the courtiers began to laugh at him. He was offered a place at the servants' table, but he refused it, saying, 'I am no ordinary donkey, I am of royal blood and must sit beside the king.'

With a laugh the king called out, 'Come here, my friend! Tell me, how do you like my daughter, the princess?'

The little donkey turned to look at her, nodded, and said,

'Indeed, I like her very much. She is the most beautiful girl I have ever set eyes on!'

'Very well, then,' said the king. 'You may have a place beside her.'

'I shall be honoured,' said the donkey.

The little donkey spent a long time at the court, but at last he said to himself, 'What is the use! I had better go home.'

Hanging his head sadly, he went to take his leave of the king. But the king had grown very fond of him, and could not bear to see him looking so sad. 'What is the matter, little donkey?' he asked. 'Stay here with me, and I will give you whatever you want. Do you need gold?'

'No,' replied the little donkey shaking his head.

'Would you like half of my kingdom?'

'No.'

Then the king said, 'If only I knew what it is you want! Would you like my daughter?'

'Oh yes,' said the little donkey, 'indeed I should.' He immediately became more cheerful, for that was exactly what he had been longing for.

The wedding was magnificent. After the feast was over, the bride and bridegroom retired to their chamber, but the king had secretly hidden one of his servants there, to make sure that the donkey treated his wife well.

The bridegroom bolted the door, looked around and, seeing no one, assumed that he and his bride were alone together. Suddenly he threw off his donkey-skin, and revealed himself as a handsome young prince.

'Now you see who I really am,' he said. 'I hope you will not feel that I am unworthy of you.'

The bride was filled with joy. She showered him with

kisses and loved him with all her heart. But next morning the prince put on his donkey-skin once more.

Soon the king came to their room and called, 'Is the little donkey awake yet?' Then he whispered to his daughter how sorry he was that she had a donkey for a husband instead of a real man.

'Oh no, dear father. I am very happy. I love him as dearly as if he were the most handsome prince in the whole world.'

The king was puzzled by this, until his servant came and told him what had happened in the royal bedroom.

'Why not hide in the room yourself, Your Majesty?' suggested the servant. 'You will see it with your own eyes, and if you throw the donkey-skin into the fire the prince will have to remain a young man!'

So that night, when the young couple were sound asleep, the king crept into their room. He saw the handsome young prince in bed, and the donkey-skin lying across a chair. He took it away and threw it into the big fire in the hall, and watched it until the last vestige had burnt away into ashes. Then he went back to the bedroom and hid behind the curtains, for he wanted to see what the young prince would do without his donkey-skin.

At first light the prince sprang out of bed and looked for the donkey-skin, but it was nowhere to be found. He turned and tried to run away, but the king was standing in the doorway.

'My son,' said the king, 'where are you going in such a hurry? You must stay with us now that you are a man.'

'Yes, I will stay,' said the prince, 'for you saw me as I really am in spite of my donkey-skin.'

The Crystal Ball

There was once a witch who had three sons. The brothers were the best of friends, but the old woman did not trust them and thought that the boys wanted to steal her magic powers. So she changed the eldest son into an eagle, who was always to be seen circling or hovering over a nearby crag. The second son she turned into a whale; but he was seen only from time to time, as he sent great spouts of sea-water gushing into the air.

The third son slipped quietly away from home, for he was afraid of being turned into a bear or a wolf. He had heard that a bewitched princess was waiting to be released from enchantment in the Castle of the Golden Sun. Anyone who tried to save her did so at the risk of his life, and already twenty-three young men had died a miserable death. Now only one more would be allowed to try. But the witch's son was fearless, and he set out to find the Castle of the Golden Sun. For many years he wandered in search of the castle, without finding it. Then one night he came to a great forest, and saw in the distance two giants beckoning to him

'Look here, young fellow,' they cried, 'we are fighting to decide which of us is to keep this hat. But as we are both equally strong neither of us can win. You look cleverer than we are. You decide!'

'Why should you quarrel over a hat?' exclaimed the lad.

'You don't know what a wonderful hat it is,' they replied. 'It is a wishing-hat! Whoever wears it can wish

to be anywhere in the whole world and will find himself there in the twinkling of an eye.'

'Give me the hat,' said the boy. 'I will take a hundred paces and, when I call you, you must run to me. Whoever reaches me first shall have the hat.'

He put the hat on his head, and walked away. But he forgot all about the two giants, for he was thinking about the bewitched princess. 'If only I were standing at the entrance to the Castle of the Golden Sun!' he sighed. No sooner had the words left his lips than he found himself on a high mountain, standing before the castle gates.

He stepped inside and went through all the rooms, until at last he found the princess. But he was aghast when he saw her, for her face was ashen grey and full of wrinkles, her eyes were dull and her hair was a violent red.

'Are *you* the princess whose beauty is famed throughout the world?' he exclaimed.

'Alas!' she cried. 'This ugly face is not my own. If you wish to see my true beauty, look into this mirror.'

She handed him the mirror, and he saw the most beautiful girl he had ever set eyes on, with tears rolling down her delicate cheeks. 'How can I set you free?' he asked. 'I will do everything in my power.'

'You must find the crystal ball,' she replied, 'and take it to the wizard. If you can do that, his power will be broken and I shall be set free. But so many young men have died already in the attempt that I am heartbroken!'

'Tell me what I must do to find the crystal ball,' he said.

'At the foot of the mountain on which this castle stands there is a spring, and near the spring you will find a wild bison. You must fight him, and if you are fortunate enough to kill him you will see a fiery bird arise in flames out of his dead body. In its beak will be a glowing egg, and the yolk of this egg is the crystal ball. The bird will not let go of the egg unless it is forced to. But if the egg falls to the ground it will burst into flames and melt away, and all your troubles will have been in vain.'

The young fellow hastened down to the spring, where he found the wild bison stamping and snorting with rage. After a long and bitter fight he ran the bison through with his sword, and the beast lay dead at his feet. Immediately the fiery bird arose out of the body, and made to fly away. But the eagle who was the boy's eldest brother was flying through the clouds overhead, and swooped on the fiery bird, chasing it out to sea. He stabbed at the bird with his beak and forced it to drop the egg. But instead of falling into the sea, the egg landed on the roof of a fisherman's hut at the water's edge.

Immediately the egg began to smoke, and it was about to burst into flames when the second brother, the whale, swam up to the beach, driving great waves, as tall as houses, before him. Water streamed over the hut and the fire was put out.

The young boy searched for the egg, and by a stroke of luck he found it. The shell was cracked and battered but the contents had not been washed away, and he took out the crystal ball unharmed.

Without wasting a moment he took it to the wizard, who said, 'My power is destroyed. You are now king of the Castle of the Golden Sun, and you have the power to restore your brothers to their human shapes.'

So the lad released his brothers and hurried to the castle, where he found the princess awaiting him in all the radiance of her true beauty. They were married, and lived happily ever after.

The Golden Goose

There was once a man who had three sons. The youngest one was called Simpleton, and everyone despised or made fun of him.

One day the eldest brother had to go into the forest for wood, and his mother gave him a cake and a bottle of wine for his midday meal.

When he came to the forest he met a little grey man,

who greeted him and said, 'I am so hungry and thirsty – please will you give me a little piece of your cake and a sip of your wine?'

'What nonsense is this?' answered the greedy boy. 'If I give away my food and drink I shall have nothing left for myself. Get out of my way!'

He began to chop a big tree with his axe, but the axe glanced off the tree-trunk and cut his arm, and he had to go home to have it bandaged. This was the work of the little grey man.

So the second son went into the forest to fetch the wood, and his mother gave him a cake and a bottle of wine for his midday meal, as she had done before. Once again the little grey man appeared and asked for a little piece of cake and a sip of wine, but the second son was as selfish as the first. 'If I give you any, I shall have less for myself,' he said. 'Go away and don't pester me!'

Punishment was not long in coming to him, for he soon chopped his leg with the axe, and had to be carried home.

'Father,' said Simpleton, 'why don't you let me go and cut the wood?'

'What is the use?' replied his father. 'Both your brothers are skilled wood-cutters, and yet they have come to grief. What do *you* know about wielding an axe?' But Simpleton persisted, until his father said, 'All right, then. I suppose you must learn the hard way!'

As he set out, his mother gave him a crust of stale bread and a bottle of sour beer to take with him. As soon as he came to the wood he met the little grey man, who said, 'Give me a piece of your cake and a drink out of your bottle. I am so hungry and thirsty!'

'I'm afraid I have only stale bread and sour beer,'

answered Simpleton. 'If that will suit you, let us eat and drink together.'

But when Simpleton brought out his stale bread it was a beautiful cake, and the sour beer had turned into the best wine. So they ate and drank together, and when they had finished the old man said, 'You are a kind lad, and willing to share whatever you have. I am going to reward you. Do you see that old tree? Cut it down, and you will find something between its roots.' And with these words the old man departed.

Simpleton rolled up his sleeves and set to work, and in no time the tree crashed to the ground. Between its roots was a goose with feathers of pure gold. He picked it up and took it to the inn where he intended to spend the night.

Now the innkeeper had three daughters, who were full of curiosity about the strange bird and thought they would each like to have one of its golden feathers.

Simpleton left his goose in the stable, and as soon as he had gone the eldest daughter crept in and seized the goose by the wing, but her hand stuck fast and she could not move it.

Soon after this the second daughter came in, also meaning to steal a feather. She fared no better, for she had barely touched her sister when she stuck fast to her.

In due course the youngest sister came in, and the other two cried, 'Take care! Keep away from us!' But the youngest sister thought they wanted to prevent her from taking a golden feather, so she tried to pull her sisters away, and – like them she stuck fast. So all three of them had to spend the night in the stable.

Next morning Simpleton came to the stable, tucked the

goose under his arm, and set off. He did not bother his head in the least about the three girls, and they were dragged along behind, unable to let go, tripping and stumbling over one another.

Halfway across a field they met the priest, who was amazed at this strange procession. 'Are you not ashamed, you silly girls, of chasing after a young fellow in this way?' he cried, and with these words he seized the youngest sister by the hand to pull her away. But the moment he touched her he, too, stuck fast, and had to hurry along behind her.

Not long after this they ran across the sexton, who was surprised to see the priest chasing after three girls. 'Where are you going in such a hurry?' he asked. 'Don't forget that we have a christening this afternoon!' He ran up to pull the priest's sleeve, and immediately stuck fast.

They had not gone far before they met two peasants, returning from work with their hatchets. The priest called out to them to come and free him and the sexton, but scarcely had they laid hands on the sexton's coat than they, too, stuck fast. Now there were seven running along behind Simpleton and his golden goose.

Some time later they came to a city where the king was in despair because his daughter was so sad. Nothing could make her smile. So he issued a proclamation that whoever could make her laugh should marry her.

Simpleton heard the proclamation, and wasted no time in parading his goose and the procession before the princess, who was so amused at this extraordinary sight that she immediately burst out laughing, till it seemed that nothing on earth could stop her. So Simpleton claimed her as his bride.

The king regretted his promise, however, and said, 'First of all you must bring me a man who can drink a whole cellar of wine in one day.'

Simpleton at once thought of the little old man in the forest, and back he went to the spot where he had felled the tree. There he saw a stranger sitting on the stump, with a face as long as a fiddle.   'What's the matter?' asked Simpleton.

'I am so thirsty!' replied the stranger. 'I cannot abide water, and I have already drunk a barrel of wine, but what is the use of such a tiny mouthful?'

'I think I can help you,' said Simpleton. 'Come with me!' And he led him to the king's cellar. The stranger set to, emptying barrel after barrel, and before the day was

out he had drunk every drop of wine in that enormous cellar.

Again Simpleton asked for his bride, but once again the king refused to keep his word, irritated by the thought that his daughter should marry a lad whom everyone called Simpleton. 'Bring me first a man who can eat a whole mountain of bread at one sitting.'

Simpleton turned and went back to the forest, followed by his long procession. Here he met another stranger, who was busy tightening a thick belt round his middle. He pulled a long face as he explained, 'I have just eaten a whole ovenful of loaves, but what is the use of such a tiny amount of bread when you are as hungry as I am? If I don't tighten my belt I shall die of starvation.'

'Come with me,' cried Simpleton. 'I think I can help you!' They found that the king had gathered together all the bread in his entire kingdom and piled it up into an enormous mountain. The stranger from the forest set to work, and before dusk he had eaten every crumb of the mountain of loaves.

For the third time Simpleton demanded his bride, but again the king refused, saying, 'Bring me a ship that can sail on both land and water. Then you may marry my daughter.'

Once again Simpleton returned to the forest, where he found his friend, the little grey man with whom he had shared his lunch. 'I have eaten for you and I have drunk for you,' said the little old man, 'and now I will give you the ship that can sail on both land and water, because you were so kind to me.'

So Simpleton sailed back to the king in his wonderful ship, and the king saw that he would have to give in and let Simpleton marry the princess, whether he liked it or not. The young couple lived happily together for many years, and after the old king's death Simpleton inherited the kingdom and became king.

Jack and the Beanstalk

There was once a poor widow who had a son called Jack and a cow called Milky-white. Their only means of livelihood was the milk which the cow gave. Every morning they took the milk to the market and sold it, until, one morning, Milky-white suddenly stopped giving milk. The poor widow thought that the end of the world had come.

'What shall we do now? What shall we do now?' she cried.

'Be brave, Mother,' said Jack. 'I will go and look for work.'

'What is the use?' said the widow. 'You tried that once before, and no one would give you a job. No, we shall have to sell Milky-white and start a shop with the money.'

'All right, Mother,' said Jack. 'Today is market-day, and I should be able to sell Milky-white for a good price.'

So Jack tied a string round the cow's neck and led her off to market. But on the way he met a strange little old man, who said, 'Good morning, Jack!'

'Good morning to you sir!' replied Jack, wondering how the old man knew his name.

'Where are you going, Jack?' asked the old man.

'I'm going to market to sell the cow.'

'I see,' said the old man. 'But you don't look clever enough to sell cows. I doubt if you can even tell me how many beans make five!'

'Oh yes, I can,' said Jack quickly. 'Two in each hand and one in your mouth.'

'Quite right,' said the old man. 'And here are the beans for you.' With these words he produced a handful of odd-looking beans from his pocket.

'Since you are so clever,' he said, 'I have no objection to doing business with you. Give me the cow, and take the beans.'

'Not so fast, not so fast!' cried Jack.

'Oh, but you don't know what wonderful beans these are,' said the man. 'If you plant them before going to bed, they will have grown right up to the sky by the morning.'

'Is that really true?' asked Jack.

'Of course it is, and if it isn't you can have your cow back again.'

'It's a bargain,' said Jack, stuffing the beans into his pocket, and handing over Milky-white's halter.

So Jack started for home and arrived well before nightfall, for there was not far to go.

His mother was most surprised to see him back so early. 'I see you have not brought Milky-white back,' she said. 'How much did you get for her?'

'You'll never guess, Mother!' he replied.

'Never guess? I shouldn't have thought it would be difficult. Five pounds? Ten? Fifteen? Surely not twenty?'

'I said you would never guess. Here – what do you think of these beans? Aren't they splendid? They are magic! If you plant them at night . . .'

'What!' cried the poor mother. 'Are you really such an idiot? Surely you did not sell our beautiful Milky-white for a handful of odd-looking beans?' And she seized the beans and threw them out of the window. 'Off to bed with you now! Not a bite of supper do you get!'

Sadly Jack climbed the stairs to his little room in the attic, sorry that his mother was so angry, and sorrier still that he had to go to bed without any supper. At last he fell asleep.

When he woke up next morning Jack felt there was something wrong. There was a bright pool of sunlight in one corner of his room, but the rest of it lay in deep shadow. He hopped out of bed and ran to the window, and what do you think he saw? The beans his mother had thrown out of the window had shot up into an enormous beanstalk, which had grown higher and higher until it reached the sky. The little old man had spoken the truth after all.

The beanstalk twined upward just outside Jack's window. He had only to open the windows and take a short step to be out on the beanstalk, which stretched up to the sky like a great ladder. He climbed and he climbed, and he climbed and he climbed, until he reached the sky. When he stepped into the sky he found himself on a long wide road which led, straight as an arrow, into the distance. Jack followed the road until he came to a big, big house, in the doorway of which stood a big, big woman.

'Good morning, good lady,' said Jack as politely as he could. 'Could you possibly let me have something for breakfast?' You will remember that Jack had been sent to bed without any supper, and by this time he was ravenous.

'You want breakfast, do you?' said the woman. 'You'll be the breakfast yourself if you don't run away quickly. My husband is a giant, and his favourite dish is roast boy on toast. He will be here immediately.'

'Please, dear lady,' begged Jack, 'give me just a morsel to eat. I have had nothing to eat since yesterday morning, and it's all the same to me whether I am roasted or starved to death.'

The giant's wife was not as bad as she seemed, for she took Jack into the kitchen and gave him a thick piece of bread and cheese and a mug of milk. But hardly had Jack begun to eat than – thud! thud! thud! – the whole house began to shake with the footsteps of the approaching giant.

'For heaven's sake, here's my husband!' cried the giant's wife. 'What can I do? Quickly, jump in here!' And she

pushed Jack into the oven just as the giant came into the room.

He was an enormous giant, bigger than any you have ever seen, and he had three calves roped to his belt. He untied a couple and threw them on to the kitchen table, saying, 'There you are, my dear. Roast me a couple for breakfast!' He sat down to wait for his meal to be cooked, but almost immediately he sniffed the air, jumped to his feet, and roared, 'What do I smell? Human flesh?'

'Nonsense, my dear,' said his wife. 'You must be dreaming – unless you can smell the remains of the tasty little boy you had for breakfast yesterday. Go and wash your hands, and your breakfast will be ready as soon as you come back.'

As soon as he had gone Jack tried to jump out of the oven and run away, but the woman said, 'Wait till he's asleep. He always takes a nap after his breakfast.'

The giant ate his two calves for breakfast; then he went to a huge chest by the wall and took out a bag of money, which he started to count. As he counted, his head began to nod until he was fast asleep, sprawled across the table. The whole house shook with his snoring.

On tiptoe Jack crept out of the oven, tucked the bag of money under his arm as he passed the giant, and ran to the top of the beanstalk as fast as his legs would carry him. He threw the sack of money into his mother's garden, and then he climbed down the beanstalk and in at his bedroom window. He told his mother all that had happened, showed her the bag of money, and said, 'Well, Mother dear, was I not right about the beans? How do you like their magic now?'

The money lasted for a long time, but in due course it

was exhausted, and Jack decided to pay the giant another visit. He rose early one fine morning and stepped out on to the beanstalk. He climbed and climbed and climbed until he found himself on the long wide road, which he followed straight to the big, big house. Once again he met the big, big woman on the doorstep.

'Good morning, good lady,' said Jack as boldly as he could. 'Can you give me a bite of breakfast?'

'Be off with you, quickly,' said the fat woman, 'or my husband will make mincemeat of you for *his* breakfast. Besides, aren't you the rascal who was here once before? Do you know anything about the bag of money my husband lost that day?'

'That's strange,' said Jack. 'Perhaps I could tell you how that happened, but at the moment I am so desperately hungry that I cannot possibly talk until I have had something to eat.'

Now the big, big woman was so curious to know what Jack had to say that she took him into the kitchen and gave him some food. But hardly had he begun his breakfast than he heard – thud! thud! thud! – the giant's footsteps approaching. Once again the giant's wife quickly bundled Jack into the oven to hide.

As he had done before, the giant stamped into the kitchen, sniffed the air and said, 'What is this I smell? Human flesh?' But his wife calmed him and gave him three roast oxen for breakfast. When he had finished, he ordered his wife to bring him his hen that laid golden eggs. So the woman brought the hen, and the giant said, 'Lay!' Immediately the hen laid an egg of pure gold.

Soon the giant began to nod and snore, and the whole house shook with the noise. Jack crept out of the oven

76

on tiptoe, seized the hen in both hands, and ran as fast as his legs would carry him. But the hen began to cackle, and the giant woke just as Jack ran out of the front door. 'Woman, woman, what have you done with my hen?' shouted the giant to his wife. 'What do you mean, my dear?' asked his wife. And that was all Jack heard, for he raced off to the beanstalk and slid quickly down it, as if he were being pursued by a dozen devils. He showed his mother the wonderful hen, and said, 'Lay!' And immediately the hen laid a golden egg.

But Jack was not satisfied. Before long he decided to try his luck with the beanstalk again. One fine morning he rose early, stepped out on to the beanstalk, and climbed and climbed and climbed until he reached the sky for a third time. He was more careful than he had been on his two other visits. Instead of going straight up the road he hid in a bush until he saw the giant's wife going to the well with a bucket. Quick as a flash, he slipped into the house and hid inside an enormous copper pan in the kitchen. Not long afterwards the house shook with the – thud! thud! thud! – of the giant coming into the kitchen with his wife. Jack cowered down inside the pan.

'What is this I smell? Human flesh?' said the giant, sniffing the air. And his wife replied, 'It must be that rascally boy who stole your money-bag and your hen. He will be hiding in the oven.'

They both rushed to the oven door, but fortunately for Jack he was not there. 'You and your "I smell human flesh!"' cried the giant's wife. 'It must be the little boy I cooked for your breakfast. After all these years you ought to be able to tell the difference between live boy and cooked boy!'

So the giant sat down to his breakfast. After a few minutes, however, he leapt to his feet, muttering, 'I could have sworn . . .' And he rummaged through the cupboard and all the drawers in the sideboard, one after the other. He looked everywhere he could think of – but luckily not inside the copper pan.

When his breakfast was finished, the giant called for his golden harp, which his wife brought and placed on the table before him. 'Sing!' he ordered, and the harp at once began to sing beautifully, and went on singing till the giant was fast asleep, and the whole house shook with his snores.

Very quietly Jack raised the lid of the pan and crept out. He crawled on all fours to the table, seized the golden harp, and fled. But the harp called out, 'Master! Master!' – and the giant jumped up just in time to see Jack disappear through the door.

Jack would very soon have been caught by the giant if he had not dodged him by running in a zig-zag, but when he came to the top of the beanstalk the giant was only ten yards behind him. Jack grasped the beanstalk and slid down it at top speed, leaving the giant wondering where he had vanished to. Suddenly the giant saw the beanstalk at his feet, but he hesitated to entrust his weight to such a slender stalk, and his hesitation gave Jack a good start. But when the golden harp again called out, 'Master! Master!' – the giant flung himself on to the beanstalk, which quivered and swayed under his weight, and began to lower himself downwards. As soon as Jack was near enough he shouted, 'Mother! Mother! Bring the axe, quickly!'

His mother came out of the house just in time to see the giant's legs dangling from the clouds, and she almost fainted away with fright. Jack leapt to the ground and seized the axe, and with one blow he cut halfway through the beanstalk. The giant could not understand why the beanstalk swayed so violently, and looked down to see what was happening. At the next blow of the axe Jack cut the stem right through, and the beanstalk toppled and broke. The giant came crashing headfirst to the ground with such force that he broke his neck, and the beanstalk fell on top of him and buried him.

Jack showed his mother the golden harp, and before long they became very rich from the harp's singing and the hen's golden eggs. Jack married a beautiful princess, and they lived happily ever after.

Myself

In a tiny little cottage in the far north, far far away from village or town, there lived a poor widow and her son, a little boy of six years old.

From their front door they could see the hills in the distance, but round about them lay nothing but moorland, giant boulders and marshy fens. Their nearest neighbours were the wee folk who lived in the mountain glens and the will-o'-the-wisps who played beside the track.

The widow could tell many strange tales of the wee folk who played in the oak trees, and of the strange lights which danced up to the windows on dark nights. But although she was lonely she had no wish to move from the little cottage, for she had no rent to pay. But she did not like staying up late at nights when the fire burned low and no one knew what was going on round about. After supper she would light a bright fire in the hearth, and creep under the bedclothes in case anything strange were to happen.

But the little boy was not at all pleased at having to go to bed so early. When his mother called him to bed, he would stay playing by the hearth, pretending not to hear.

He had always been a difficult child, ever since he had been born. The more his mother insisted on obedience, the less attention he would pay her, and he generally finished by having his own way.

One evening, however, when winter was almost over, the widow did not want to leave her child playing alone by the fire. The wind was tearing at the door and rattling the window-panes, and she knew well enough that it was on just such a night that the elves and fairies liked to play their pranks. So she tried to persuade the little boy to go to bed.

'It is safest in bed on a night like this,' she said. But still he would not do as he was told. She threatened him with the stick, but in vain. She scolded him and coaxed him, but it was no use: he refused to go to bed. At last she lost patience with him, and said, 'Very well then – I hope the wicked fairies take you away!' He laughed, and said he hoped they would, for he had been wanting someone to play with for a long time.

His poor mother lay down in despair, certain that something dreadful was going to happen. Meantime her thoughtless little boy sat on a stool by the fire. He did not sit long alone, for suddenly he heard a strange fluttering in the chimney, and a tiny little girl – the neatest, sweetest little thing you can imagine – came floating down the

chimney and landed on the hearth. She was only a few inches high, her hair was like spun silver, her eyes as green as grass, and her cheeks pink as June roses.

The little boy looked at her with wide eyes. 'Oh!' he said in astonishment. 'Who are you?'

'Myself,' she replied, in a high-pitched but sweet little voice. 'And who are you?'

'I am myself too,' he replied with caution, and the two began to play with each other.

The tiny creature showed him a great many fine games. She made animals out of ashes, which moved and looked alive, and trees with quivering green leaves beside tiny cottages with tiny men and women, who moved and spoke as soon as she breathed on them.

By this time the fire had died down, and there was only a faint glow in the ashes. So the boy took a stick and poked the embers to make them burn up, and that is how it came about that a red-hot coal leapt out of the fire and landed – where do you think? – right on the fairy child's foot! She set up such a loud crying that the little boy dropped the stick and clasped both hands to his ears. But the cry grew to a shriek, as if all the winds of the world were being forced through a tiny keyhole.

Once again there was a strange fluttering in the chimney, but this time the little boy did not wait to see what it was. He dived head first into bed. Slowly his head emerged from beneath the quilt, as he waited, petrified, to see what would happen.

A high-pitched, piercing voice came down the chimney, 'Who is it, and what's the matter?'

'It is I, Myself,' sighed the fairy child. 'My foot is burnt and very sore.'

'Who did it?' asked the angry voice in the chimney. This time it sounded closer, and the little boy, peeping out from under the bedclothes, could see a pale white face in the chimney opening.

'Myself,' replied the fairy girl.

'Well if you did it yourself, what is all the fuss about?' cried the fairy mother. And she stretched out a long thin arm and seized the little girl by the ear, shook her roughly above the embers, and drew her up the chimney.

For a long time the little boy lay awake, in case the fairy mother should come back for him.

Next evening, to his mother's great surprise, he made no fuss about going to bed when he was told. 'At last he is becoming obedient,' his mother said to herself. But her son was thinking that he certainly would not be let off so lightly if the fairy came to play with him again.

The Little Shepherd Boy

There was once a little shepherd who was renowned for the clever answers he gave to any question that was put to him. The king of the country heard about him and sent for him, in order to test his powers.

'If you can answer my three questions,' said the king, 'I will take you as my own child, to live with me here in the palace.'

'As you wish,' replied the boy. 'What are your questions?'

'Here is the first,' said the king. 'How many drops of water are there in the sea?'

'Your Majesty,' replied the boy, 'if you will block up all the rivers in the world, so that not a drop more water can flow into the sea, then I will tell you how many drops there are in it.'

'Here is the second question,' said the king. 'How many stars are there in the sky?'

'Give me a big sheet of paper,' said the boy. Then he took a pen and marked so many dots on the paper that it was impossible to distinguish one dot from the next, and it made the king quite giddy just to look at it. 'There are as many stars in the sky as there are dots on this paper,' said the boy. 'Count them!' But no one was able to count them.

'Here, then, is my third question,' said the king. 'How many seconds are there in eternity?'

'That's easy,' replied the boy. 'There is a huge mountain called Diamond Mountain, twenty thousand feet high and twenty miles round. Once every hundred years a sparrow comes and sharpens its beak on this mountain. When the whole mountain has been worn away, that will be the end of the first second of eternity.'

'Good,' said the king. 'You have answered my questions with the wisdom of a great scholar. You shall stay in my palace, and I will look on you as my own child.'

The Dancing Princesses

There was once a king who had twelve daughters, each one more beautiful than the next. They slept together in a room where their beds were arranged in a long line. Every night when they went to bed the king locked the door from the outside, yet every morning their shoes were worn out with dancing, and no one could discover how this could happen.

At length the king proclaimed that whoever could discover where the princesses danced every night would be allowed to marry any one of his daughters he chose, and would become king of the land after his death. But anyone who made the attempt, and failed to solve the problem within three days and three nights, would forfeit his life.

Not long afterwards a prince came forward. He was well received, and in the evening was conducted to a bedroom next to the room where the princesses slept. In this way he thought he would have little difficulty in discovering where they went to dance. The doors of both bedrooms were left open all night, so that he would see if the girls left their room. But the prince's eyelids felt like lead, and he fell fast asleep. Next morning, when he awoke, all the princesses had been out dancing for there were holes in the soles of their shoes. Exactly the same happened on the second and third nights, and the prince had to forfeit his life.

A great many young princes made the attempt, but none succeeded in solving the problem.

One day a poor soldier, who had been wounded and was unable to serve in the army any more, was on his way back from the wars when he met an old woman who asked him where he was going. 'I am not sure,' he said, and added as a joke, 'Perhaps I shall find out where the princesses dance, and then become king!'

'That is not so very difficult,' said the old woman. 'You must be careful not to drink the wine which you will be offered at bedtime, and at night you must pretend to be fast asleep.' Then she handed him a red cloak, saying, 'If you wear this you will be invisible, and so be able to follow the twelve princesses without being seen.'

The soldier decided to try his luck, so he went to the king and announced himself as a suitor for one of his daughters. At bed-time he was taken to his room, and just as he was going to bed the eldest princess brought him a goblet of wine. But he had hidden a sponge in his shirt, and he poured all the wine down his neck into the sponge, without swallowing a single drop. Then he lay down, and soon began to snore as if he were sound asleep.

The twelve princesses heard the snoring and laughed. 'What a pity that these men insist on throwing away their lives like this!' said one of them. Then they got out of bed and in next to no time they had changed into their best dresses, and were preening and primping in front of their mirrors, skipping about in excited anticipation of the

dance – all but the youngest princess, who said, 'I don't know why it is, but I feel so strange. I am sure there is trouble in store for us tonight.'

'You are always worrying!' said one of her sisters. 'Don't you remember how many young men have tried to follow us already? Even without the sleeping-draught the soldier would probably have slept till morning.'

When they were all ready, the eldest princess tapped three times on the end of her bed. Immediately it sank into the floor, and the princesses descended through the opening, one after the other, led by the eldest.

Meantime the soldier, who had been watching through his lashes, put on his red cloak and went down through the hole behind the youngest princess. Halfway down he trod on the hem of her dress. She was terrified and cried, 'Who's that? Who is holding my dress?' 'Don't be so simple,' said the eldest sister. 'You must have caught it on a nail.'

When they came to the bottom they found themselves in a magnificent wide avenue bordered by trees with leaves of real silver, which gleamed and shimmered in the moonlight. To prove that he had been there, the soldier

broke off a twig to take back with him. There was a loud crack. 'Did you hear that?' cried the youngest princess. 'I tell you, there is something wrong tonight!'

'Nonsense!' said the eldest. 'The princes must be celebrating our arrival with fireworks.'

Soon they came to an avenue bordered by trees with leaves of pure gold, and finally to an avenue where the leaves were of diamonds. In each of the tree-walks the soldier broke off a twig, and each time there was a loud crack, which made the youngest princess jump with fright. But the eldest princess still insisted that it must be fireworks.

On they went until they came to a lake where twelve little boats were waiting. In each of them sat a handsome prince, waiting to take one of the princesses. The soldier stepped into the boat with the youngest princess, and the prince who was rowing her said, 'I do not know what is the matter tonight. The boat feels much heavier than usual. It is far more difficult to row.'

On the far side of the lake stood a beautiful, bright castle, from which came the sounds of violins and flutes. They rowed to the shore below the castle, and each prince led his princess inside and danced with her.

The dancing went on till three in the morning, when the princesses' shoes were quite worn out. The princes rowed them back across the lake, and this time the soldier sat in the first boat with the eldest princess. On the other shore the sisters took their leave of the princes and promised to return on the following night.

When they reached the stairs the soldier ran on in front, and by the time the tired princesses had climbed slowly up to their room he was lying snoring on his bed. They put their fine clothes away and went to sleep, leaving the worn-out shoes beneath their beds.

Next morning the soldier said nothing, for he wanted to watch the twelve sisters again. He followed them on the second and third nights, and everything happened exactly as on the first occasion – but on the third night he brought back a wine-glass with him as proof.

When it was time to give his answer to the question, the soldier took the wine-glass and the three twigs and went before the king, while the princesses hid behind the door and listened. 'Where have my daughters worn out their shoes?' asked the king. 'They dance each night with twelve princes in an underground castle,' replied the soldier. He described to the king exactly what had happened, and produced his evidence.

The king called for his daughters and asked if the soldier had spoken the truth. They confessed everything, for they saw it was no use denying the story.

'Which of my daughters will you choose for your bride?' asked the king.

'I am no longer young,' replied the soldier. 'Give me the eldest.'

So they were married the same day, and the soldier was promised the kingdom after the king's death. But the princes were put under a spell for as many days as the number of nights they had spent dancing with the twelve beautiful sisters.

The Sorcerer and his Apprentice

A poor woman was once going through a dark wood with her youngest son, Jack. Tears were streaming down her cheeks, for she had many children but lacked the means to feed and educate them all.

Suddenly a man, who had been sitting at the foot of a great oak tree, rose to his feet and asked her why she was crying, so she told him of her troubles. The stranger comforted her and said he was a tailor, and would willingly take young Jack into apprenticeship for three years. But he was lying, for he was not a tailor but a sorcerer. Jack's mother had no means of knowing this, and went off home rejoicing, leaving Jack with the sorcerer, who took him by the hand and led him to a great cave. Here Jack was set to learn the black arts, and before long he was more powerful than his master.

One day towards the end of the third year, Jack escaped from the sorcerer's cave and hurried to see his mother, who wept tears of joy to see him so big and strong and well. 'In a week, Mother dear,' said Jack, 'my three years will be up and you must come to my master and claim me back. He will show you a flock of doves and ask which of them is your son; for the doves are not really doves, but young boys whom he took into apprenticeship and bewitched. When he scatters peas before the doves, look for the only dove which does not eat, but flutters his wings with joy. That will be your son.'

A week later the mother went to the sorcerer and asked for her son. The old fellow took out a copper trumpet and sounded it in all directions, and at once a vast cloud of doves converged on them. The sorcerer scattered peas before the doves, and told the woman to pick out her son. All the birds seemed to be busy on the ground pecking at the peas, but one dove alone fluttered about without landing. The woman pointed to this dove, and the sorcerer had to release her son.

Jack was now a highly skilled wizard. 'I know how to make you rich,' he said to his father, who was a poor cobbler, 'but it cannot be done all at once. I will change myself first into a cow, then into a bullock, and then into a sheep. Each time you must take me to the market and sell me. The money will be yours, but I will leave the animal form with the buyer and come back to you in my own form. But you must be very careful never to wish that I were a horse, for if you do I shall be in great danger, and shall lose my power to help you.'

So the cobbler made a great deal of money from the sale of a cow, a bullock, and a sheep. He was able to buy himself a new cottage, and there was no longer any shortage of food in the house. But then he grew greedy, and in spite of Jack's warning he wished his poor son into a horse, and led him to market. The sorcerer was already waiting there to buy the horse, and he paid even more for it than the cobbler asked.

Once again the sorcerer had Jack in his power. He took him to a stable where he chained him up, with nothing to eat or drink, and beat him severely with a whip until the poor horse was black and blue. The sorcerer's servant-lass took pity on him, and went into his stall to feed him. As soon as she unfastened his chain Jack took on his natural form, thanked the girl for helping him, and flew on to the

roof in the form of a sparrow, afraid that his master would find him.

The sorcerer, however, recognized Jack in the sparrow and, turning himself into an enormous black crow, he swooped on the poor little bird. Jack flew as fast as he could, but the crow pursued him closely. At length he fell almost dead with exhaustion into a bush in the king's garden. The furious crow was about to pounce on him when he turned into a little wren. But then the sorcerer changed himself into a sparrow, and so the hunt went on.

At that moment the king's daughter, who was strolling in the garden, saw the struggle between the two birds.

'How dreadful!' she cried out in dismay. 'Why must even the smallest creatures fight?'

By this time Jack was quite exhausted, and could no longer hope to escape from the angry sparrow, so he changed himself into a beautiful ring on the princess's little finger. The sparrow searched for him everywhere, until at last he realized what Jack had done – but still he would not give up the fight.

The princess had returned to her room before she noticed with wonder the strange ring on her finger; but in the same instant Jack changed again, and stood before her in his own form. He explained what had happened, and warned her of the sorcerer, who would undoubtedly come to the palace and ask for the ring. 'If he lays hands on me', he added, 'all will be lost. The best thing will be for you to throw the ring on the floor as hard as you can if the sorcerer is too persistent.'

Just as he feared, the sorcerer came to the palace next day, disguised as a prince, with many servants. No sooner had the princess been presented to him than he asked to see the ring. In the meantime, however, Jack had won the princess's love, and she would not show the sorcerer her hand. But when he continued to pester her, she slipped the ring from her finger and hurled it violently to the ground. Immediately thousands of peas were rolling about the floor, but there was no ring to be seen.

The sorcerer took out his copper trumpet and blew a strange note in all directions, and a cloud of doves swooped down and began to devour the peas. But the princess had concealed a single pea in the palm of her hand. She hurled it to the ground, and out of the pea fell thousands of tiny black poppy seeds.

Again the sorcerer put his trumpet to his lips and blew a different note, and hundreds of sparrows flew down from all directions. In order to waste no time in pecking up the poppy seeds the sorcerer turned himself into a sparrow.

This was just what Jack had been waiting for. In the twinkling of an eye he turned himself into a great black crow, and bit off the wicked sorcerer's head.

The princess took Jack for her husband, and they celebrated their wedding with a magnificent feast, at which the eating and drinking and dancing went on well into the night.

The Princess under the Earth

There was once a wealthy king, who married, and soon became the father of the most beautiful of daughters. When this daughter was seventeen he shut her in a magnificent palace built specially for her under the earth. Then he sent messengers to the four points of the compass to announce that the first young man to find his daughter could have her as his bride; but whoever made the attempt and failed would forfeit his life.

Many fine young men tried, but each one failed and paid with his life, until at last a certain clever and handsome young man decided to make the attempt. He went to a shepherd, saying, 'Will you conceal me in a fleece of gold and take me to the king?'

The shepherd agreed and sewed the young man carefully into a golden lamb's fleece so that he looked just like a golden lamb. Then he took him to the king, who was so pleased with the lamb that he offered to buy it.

'No, Your Majesty,' said the shepherd, 'I'm afraid that is impossible. I am quite prepared to *lend* it to you for three days if you wish, but you must promise to give it back to me.'

The king promised, and took the lamb to show it to the princess. He passed through a great many rooms in the palace, until at last he came to a heavy iron door. He gave a special knock, and commanded, 'Open wide, you portals of the earth!' Immediately the door creaked open. Once again he passed through a great many rooms, until he came to a second heavy iron door, to which he cried, 'Open wide, you portals of the earth!'

When this door creaked open, he found himself in a room where the walls were of purest silver. This was where his daughter, the princess, lived, the most beautiful girl in the whole world. She was delighted with the golden lamb, and stroked and caressed it.

During the night, when the princess was alone, the young fellow slipped out of the lambskin and stood before the princess. As soon as she set eyes on him she fell in love. 'How clever you are!' she cried. 'But you have not won yet, for my father will set you a more difficult task. He will change me and all my ladies into ducks, and then he will ask you which duck is the princess. Listen carefully, and I will tell you how to recognize me. I shall be the duck which turns its head round to preen its wing feathers.'

After three days the shepherd went to the king to ask for his lamb back. The princess was sorry to lose it, but the king explained that he had promised to return it to the shepherd.

So the lamb went away with the shepherd, but as soon as they were out of sight of the palace the young man shed his lambskin and went straight back to the king. 'Your Majesty,' he said, 'I should like to seek for your daughter.' The king was greatly impressed by the young man's bearing, and felt sorry for him. 'Consider well what you are doing, my boy, for it will probably mean your death!'

'No,' persisted the boy, 'I will find her or die in the attempt.'

So he set out, and the king followed behind him. When they came to the first door, the young fellow said, 'Your Majesty, you must say seven words now.'

'What seven words?' asked the king.

'You must say, "Open wide, you portals of the earth!"'

The door opened at once, and the king began to gnaw his beard with misgiving. The second door opened just as the first had done, and they found themselves in the princess's superb silver room.

'Very well,' said the king. 'You have found my daughter, but she is not yours yet.' And all at once the princess and all her ladies turned into ducks. 'Now,' said the king, 'show me which one is the princess!'

One of the ducks was preening its wing feathers with its beak, and the young man pointed to it without hesitation, saying, 'That one is the princess!'

So the king was forced to give up his daughter, and the two young people were married the same day, and lived happily together.

Foxglove

There was once a poor hunchback who lived in the fertile valley of Acherlow, at the foot of gloomy Galtymore in southern Ireland. The great hump on his back made him look as if his body had moved up on to his shoulders, and the local people were scared of meeting him in a lonely place, although he was quite harmless and the soul of kindness.

His deformity was so great, however, that he hardly looked like a man at all, and some malicious people had spread strange stories about him. He was said to have an extraordinary knowledge of herbs and magic, but the only certain fact was that he was highly skilled at weaving baskets out of straw and reeds, and in this way he earned his livelihood.

People had given him the name of Foxglove, for in his hat he always used to wear a sprig of the red foxglove called Elf's Cap. His basket-work generally brought him in more money than other basket-makers earned, and the envy of one or two of them must have been at the root of all the weird and wonderful stories that were told about him.

Now it happened that Foxglove was on the way home late one night, for his progress was slow on account of the hump on his back, and it was already dark by the time he had to pass the ancient burial mound of Knockgrafton. Worn out and tired he sat down to rest on the edge of the mound, and looked miserably at the silver disc of the rising moon.

All at once a strange, subterranean music reached poor Foxglove's ears, and he thought he had never heard anything so lovely. It was as if many voices were singing together in such perfect harmony that, at times, it seemed almost as if there were only one voice. He could pick out the words clearly enough: 'Da luan, da mort, da luan, da mort, da luan, da mort.' Then there would be a short pause before the same song started up again.

Foxglove listened carefully, scarcely daring to breathe for fear that he should miss any of the singing. It was clear to him that the sound came from inside the mound, and so, when the next pause came in the singing, he took up the melody, using his own words: 'Augus da cadine, augus da cadine.' Then he joined in the chorus of 'Da luan, da mort,' and again sang, 'Augus da cadine,' in the pause that followed.

The tiny singers inside the mound were thrilled at this addition to their song, and decided to fetch this mortal, whose musical gifts so far exceeded their own, to sing with them underground. With the breathless speed of a whirlwind Foxglove was carried down to them, and he found himself in an underground chamber, into which he came circling as lightly as a straw in the wind. Finally he was set down amongst the musicians, and servants were appointed to bring him whatever he wanted to eat or drink. But when he noticed that the elves were all busily whispering together and glancing at him out of the corners of their eyes, he began to be a little frightened. One of the tiniest elves came up to him, and said:

> 'Foxglove, Foxglove,
> Be of good cheer!
> Take off your hump
> And lay it down here.'

Scarcely had the little elf finished speaking than Foxglove felt so light that he could have leapt over the moon, just like the cow in the story of the cat and the fiddle. He was overjoyed to see his hump rolling about on the floor in front of him, and to feel his back as straight and as strong as any young man's in the whole valley. Shyly he looked about him at the sea of elfin faces, and he was so overwhelmed at the warmth and friendliness of his reception that his head began to swim. His dazzled eyes closed and he collapsed into a deep sleep.

It was full daylight when he awoke to find himself lying on the mound in bright sunshine, while the birds sang and the sheep and cows grazed peacefully around him. Thinking it had all been a dream he felt his back, but there was no trace of his hump! Full of pride, he looked at himself. He was dressed from head to foot in fine new clothes! Undoubtedly he had the wee spirits to thank for it all.

He said his prayers and set out for Acherlow, feeling so light on his feet that he gave a little hop and a skip every now and then, as if he had been doing it all his life. No one who met him recognized Foxglove, and he had the greatest difficulty in convincing the people who he really was.

As is always the way, the story of Foxglove's hump spread throughout the whole valley, and soon everyone, rich and poor, was talking of nothing else.

One morning Foxglove was sitting at his front door, feeling very pleased with life, when a wizened old woman approached him. 'Can you show me the way to Acherlow?' she asked.

'There is no need,' he replied. 'This is Acherlaw. But, tell me, where have you come from?'

'I have come from Waterford, and I am looking for a man called Foxglove, who had a hump removed from his shoulders by the elves. My friend has a son with an enormous hump on his back, and I thought I might help him to get rid of it if I could only learn something of the magic Foxglove used. Now perhaps you will realize why I have come so far. I want, if I can, to learn magic.'

So Foxglove – who was always eager to help others – told the old woman how he had heard the singing of the elves inside the mound, how he had joined in, how he had been carried underground, and how the elves had taken the hump from his shoulders.

The old woman thanked him a thousand times, and set off for home.

Some days later she came to her poor friend in Waterford, and related the whole story to her, exactly as she had heard it from Foxglove. Then she lifted the little hunchback, who had been mean and malicious all his life, into a cart and set off to the mountains.

It was a long, long way, but what did that matter if he could lose his hump, they thought.

They trudged on for several days along the rough road to Acherlow and the burial mound of Knockgrafton, pushing the rickety cart with its heavy burden before them and pausing only now and then to take a little food and drink or to sleep for an hour. As the two women struggled and panted, the hunchback muttered and grumbled, cursing them for their slowness. His temper had never been sweet, and now it was soured entirely by the discomfort of his hard and bumpy ride.

Why couldn't the two old hags move faster? And why should he have to travel so far in order to be rid of his hump?

On the fifth day at nightfall they reached the mound, and the old woman lifted the hunchback out of the cart, and set him down on the ground.

Jack Madden – for that was the hunchback's name – had not long to wait before he heard the music coming from the mound beneath him, but it was sweeter than ever now, for the elves had added to their song the refrain they had learnt from Foxglove: 'Da luan, da mort, da luan, da mort, da luan, da mort, augus da cadine.'

Jack, whose only thought was to lose his hump as quickly as possible, did not bother to wait for the elves to finish singing, nor did he wait for a suitable pause in the song, but burst in at the top of his voice and quite out of tune: 'Augus dia dardine, augus da hena.' He thought that if Foxglove had been rewarded for one extra phrase he would be doubly rewarded for two.

Scarcely had the words left his lips than he felt himself being lifted up and dragged roughly into the mound. He found himself surrounded by a ring of elves, who were screaming angrily, 'Who has spoilt our song? Who has ruined our melody?' Then one of them stepped forward and said:

> 'Jack Madden, Jack Madden,
> You sing like a crow!
> Where now you have one hump
> A second must grow!'

Twenty of the strongest elves dragged out Foxglove's hump and placed it on top of the miserable Jack Madden's own, and there it stuck fast as if it had been nailed on by a joiner or a blacksmith.

Then the elves kicked him out of the mound, and when his mother and her friend came for him next morning they found him lying half dead on the hillside, with a second hump on his back. For a while they stared at him, and were soon frightened that the elves might give him a third hump out of spite. So they lifted him on to the cart and wheeled him home as quickly as possible. It was a sad sight to see.

Not long after this Jack died, weighed down and exhausted by his two humps, and as he died he cursed anyone who ever heard the singing of the elves again.

The Months

There were once two brothers, of whom the elder was called Gianni and the younger Eliseo. Gianni led a life of luxury and idleness, while Eliseo was as poor as a church mouse. Gianni was as mean as he was rich, and would have allowed his brother to starve to death rather than lend him a farthing.

His poverty drove Eliseo to leave home and seek his fortune. One evening, after a long and arduous journey, he arrived at an inn where there were twelve guests, apart from himself. They made a space for him by the fire, and he was glad to go and sit with them, for he was freezing.

They soon got talking and one of the twelve strangers, whose fierce, gloomy features made him quite terrifying to look at, asked him, 'What do you think of this weather, my friend?'

'What can one think of it?' replied Eliseo. 'I think that each month of the year does its proper duty. We have the impertinence to find fault with natural laws, without having any notion of what is good for us. In winter, when it is cold, we complain that it is not warmer. In the heat of summer we want to be cool. If the weather were always to do what *we* wanted, the seasons would be topsy-turvy, seeds would not germinate properly, the harvest would be ruined, people would gradually die off, and the whole world would fall into confusion. Let the seasons take their natural course. After all, we have the trees to give us fuel in winter and shade in summer.'

'You sound as wise as Solomon,' said the man, 'but you can hardly deny that this month of March is a pretty miserable one, with its rain and frost, snow and hail, gales and storms, fogs and drizzle. March can make life very miserable for us.'

'You are listing only the bad things about March,' replied Eliseo. 'Why do you say nothing of the good things? After all, does not March herald the spring? Does it not begin the growth that will end in a fruitful harvest?'

The stranger was delighted at these words, for he was none other than the month of March himself, who happened to be spending the night at the inn with his eleven brothers. To reward Eliseo for his kind words he gave him a little box, saying. 'You will find everything you need in this box. Whenever you want anything, just open it.'

Eliseo thanked March for his kindness and used the box as a pillow when he lay down to sleep. Early next morning he said goodbye to the twelve months, and set off for home.

The day was cold and the snow lay deep on the ground. Eliseo opened the box and said, 'If only I had a sedan chair, cushioned in soft, warm silk, so that I should not have to wade through all this snow!'

Hardly had the words left his lips when a sedan chair appeared with its two bearers, who lifted him in and set off for his home.

When he grew hungry, he opened the box and said, 'I wish I had something to eat!' He was immediately surrounded by the most sumptuous dishes – more than enough for ten people.

Late in the evening they came to a forest where he decided to spend the night. He wished himself a large tent of oiled canvas, and a four-poster bed spread with beautifully soft, warm quilts. His supper was delicious and the aroma spread far and wide throughout the forest.

Next morning he took the lid off the box, with the words, 'I wish for such magnificent clothes that my brother will be green with envy when he sees me!' Immediately he was clad in a cloak of heavy black velvet embroidered with scarlet thread.

A few hours later he arrived at his brother's house.

believe his eyes when he saw Eliseo
G. chair and so magnificently dressed,
wanted to know how his brother could
les. So Eliseo told him about the twelve
inn, who had rewarded him so richly. He
however, not to disclose the conversation
had with the month of March.

ld hardly wait to show Eliseo out of the
on as he was alone he set off for the inn, where
twelve brothers, just as Eliseo had done. He
down on a seat amongst them without so much
sked, and started to complain about the dreadful

evil take this wretched month of March!' he
drives farmers to despair, and it makes us all ill
ughly miserable. The winds chill our bones, the
now kill the seeds in the soil. In short, it would
g for the whole world if March could be elimin-
ated altogether.'

March, who could not help the way he was made,
concealed his displeasure at this rude criticism, and next
morning he gave Gianni a fine strong threshing flail just as
he was departing for home, saying, 'Whenever you want
anything, all you need to do is to say. "Threshing flail,
give me a hundred", and you will get a tremendous surprise!'

Gianni thanked March for his present, and hurried home
as quickly as he could, for he wanted to try out the magic
power of the threshing flail in his own home where no one
would see him. As soon as he arrived at his house he shut
himself up in the cellar, where he intended to store all the
gold he expected to receive, and said, 'Threshing flail, give

me a hundred!' And the flail gave him far more than a hundred! It beat him all over, on arms, legs, head, and body, till he was black and blue from head to foot. Even then it did not stop, but luckily for Gianni his brother Eliseo heard his groans and shouts for help. He hurried to the rescue at once, and stopped the threshing flail with the aid of his magic box.

When Gianni had sufficiently recovered from the pain and shock, he began to complain bitterly at the conduct of the twelve brothers at the inn.

'You have only yourself to blame,' said Eliseo. 'You brought this punishment on yourself through your own stupidity. Your rudeness is the sole cause of your misfortune. Why can you not keep a courteous tongue in your head? If you had been polite to the months, you would have been well rewarded. It costs nothing to be polite, and it can bring unexpected rewards, as you have seen.'

To comfort his elder brother, Eliseo forgave him all his meanness in the past, and offered to share the magic box with him in the future. For the box could easily have filled the houses of a hundred misers with gold, and God had intended all the good things of this world to be shared, in any case.

Gianni told Eliseo how sorry he was that he had behaved so badly, and the two brothers lived together from that time onward in peace and happiness, sharing all their possessions equally.

King Golden

Many long years ago a poor shepherd built a little hut in a dense forest, and there he lived with his wife and six sons. The children used to take water from the well and fruit from the garden to their father when he was out tending the sheep.

The youngest son was called Golden Boy, for his hair gleamed in the sunlight like beaten gold. Although he was the youngest, he was bigger and stronger than any of his brothers. When the children were out in the woods, Golden Boy would lead the way with a stout cudgel in his hand and his brothers would follow him through the thickest and darkest parts of the forest, even when it was growing dark and the moon was already shining above the mountains.

They were returning home late one evening, so engrossed in their game that they thought Golden Boy's hair was the setting sun.

'We must hurry,' said the eldest. 'It will soon be dark.'

'Look!' cried the second brother. 'There's the moon!'

A light suddenly streamed between the dark pine trees, and a strange woman, gleaming silver like the moon, could be seen sitting on a mossy boulder, spinning a fine thread on a crystal spindle. She nodded her head to Golden Boy, and sang:

> 'The snow-white finch – the golden rose,
> The crown beneath the ocean glows.'

Then the fine thread snapped and her song broke off. Her light was snuffed like a candle.

A strange fear filled the six brothers, and they soon lost one another as they made their way over boulders and clambered over hillocks in the dark.

Golden Boy wandered about all that night and the following day without finding any trace of his brothers or of his parents, or of any other human being. The forest had become very dense, and was full of hillocks separated by deep ravines. He would have been very hungry and thirsty, had it not been for the wild brambles which grew over everything.

At last, after many days, the trees began to thin out and it grew lighter. At last Golden Boy found himself in a pleasant meadow where he felt he could breathe more freely.

Laid out on the meadow he saw a great many nets. 'They must belong to a fowler, who catches birds as they fly out of the wood and sells them in the city,' he thought.

The fowler, however, was hiding behind a nearby bush and said to himself, 'He seems a fine young lad. I can use him!' He pulled a string, and suddenly Golden Boy found himself entangled in a net. He was taken completely by surprise and lay on the ground, wondering what had happened.

'This is how we catch birds!' shouted the fowler with a laugh. 'Your golden feathers will be most useful to me. Stay here with me, and I will teach you how to catch birds.'

Golden Boy liked the idea of living in the woods amongst the birds, and agreed to stay, though he had not altogether given up hope of returning home.

'Show me what you have learnt,' said the fowler a few days later. So Golden Boy pulled on his net, and caught a tiny, snow-white finch, which he handed to his master. In a rage, the fowler flung the little bird to the ground, and trampled it to death. 'Away you go!' he shouted furiously at Golden Boy. 'You must be in league with the devil!'

Golden Boy could not understand why the fowler was so angry, and wandered on through the forest, looking for his father's house. He slept under a boulder the first night, and under the roots of a fallen tree on the second night, and by day he struggled onwards through the undergrowth, stumbling over roots and sinking into patches of bog.

On the third day the forest began to thin out and it grew lighter, and he found himself in a beautiful garden full of flowering trees and shrubs. Flowers bloomed all round him, and Golden Boy gazed at them in wonder. He had stopped beneath a huge sun-flower, which glowed the same colour as his own hair in the sunlight. The gardener saw him and shouted, 'Hey, young fellow, come here! I can use you!'

Golden Boy agreed to work in the garden, for he thought life amongst the flowers would be very pleasant – though he still hoped to find his way home before long.

One day the gardener sent him into the forest to find a wild briar for grafting new roses. He soon returned with a briar bearing the most beautiful golden roses, which looked as if they had been wrought out of gold by the most skilful goldsmith for the royal table.

'You and your golden roses!' yelled the gardener in a fury. 'You must be in league with the devil himself!' And he chased Golden Boy out of the garden, and trampled the beautiful roses underfoot.

Golden Boy could not understand why the gardener was so angry, and wandered off into the forest to look for his father's hut. Day and night he stumbled over mossy boulders and fallen tree-trunks, until on the third day the forest became lighter and the trees thinned out, and he found himself on the seashore. The water stretched away into the distance as far as his eyes could see, its mirror-bright surface reflecting the golden sunlight so that it was like a sea of liquid gold. On it a number of sailing-ships decorated with long, flowing pennants were gliding. In a rowing-boat on the shore sat a group of fishermen, who beckoned to Golden Boy to join them.

'You're just the person we've been looking for!' they said, as they pushed off from the shore, and Golden Boy gazed with pleasure at the scintillating water all around him. This would be a fine life, he thought, but he had not yet given up hope of finding his father's house.

The fisher-folk threw out their nets, but caught nothing. 'Let's see if you will have any more luck!' said an old, white-haired fisherman. Golden Boy cast the net awkwardly into the water. He pulled it in, and fished out – a crown of pure gold.

'All hail to our new king!' cried the old fisherman, and fell on his knees before him. 'Over a hundred years ago our last king threw his crown into the sea, saying that the kingdom should belong to the man who recovered the crown from the depths.'

'All hail to our new king!' repeated the other fisher-folk, as they set the crown on Golden Boy's head.

The news of the crown quickly spread from ship to ship,

far across the water until it reached the land. Soon the whole shimmering sea was covered with boats and ships, and the people came to greet their new king with shouts of jubilation.

Beauty

Once upon a time there was a poor couple who lived in a tiny house. They had one child, a daughter, who was as beautiful and kind as could be. She worked hard, sweeping and washing, spinning and sewing, and those who lived round about called her Beauty, because of her fine and lovely features. But because people stared so when they saw her beautiful face, she became shy and wore a veil on Sundays when she went to church.

One fine Sunday the king's son was passing through the village and caught a glimpse of Beauty on her way to church. He immediately fell in love with her graceful figure, as slender as a young pine, but he was sorry he could not see her face through the veil. 'Why does Beauty keep her face covered?' he asked his servant.

'Because she is so modest,' the servant replied.

There and then the prince made up his mind to marry Beauty, and to love her all his life. 'Go to her,' he ordered his servant, 'and give her this gold ring from me. Tell her I should like to speak to her, and that I will wait for her beside the great oak tree at sunset.'

The attendant did as he was told, but Beauty thought that the prince wanted nothing more than to order some embroidery from her, so she went to the great oak tree at sunset. How surprised she was when the prince declared his love, and asked her to be his wife. She replied with modesty and humility, 'I am a poor girl and you are a rich prince. Your father would be very angry if he knew you wanted to marry me.'

But the prince was most persistent, and Beauty at last agreed to think it over if he would allow her a few days in which to do so. But the prince could not wait for a few days, and the very next morning he sent his servant to Beauty's house with a pair of silver shoes, asking her to meet him once again beneath the great oak tree.

As soon as she arrived at the oak he asked her if she had made up her mind, but she replied that she had not had time, for she had so much work to do at home. In any case, she was only a poor girl and he was a rich prince, and his father would be furious if he married her. But the prince persisted, until she promised to speak to her parents about the matter.

Next day the prince sent her a beautiful dress of glittering gold, and asked her once again to meet him by the great oak tree. When she arrived at the tree he asked her if she had made up her mind. Once again she gave the same reply – that she had too much work to do, and had not had any time to consider – and repeated that it was most unsuitable for a rich prince to marry such a poor girl, and that the king his father would be furious if he knew. But the prince insisted that she should become his bride, and should later become queen, whatever his father might think. Beauty saw that the prince really meant what he said, and from now on they met every evening at sunset under the great oak. For the present, however, the king was to be kept in ignorance of their engagement.

Now there was at the royal court a malicious old woman who had been spying on the prince, and when she discovered his secret she told the king all about it. The king was indeed furious, and sent his men-at-arms to set fire to the little house where Beauty's parents lived. They perished in the blaze, poor folk, but Beauty managed to escape through a window and climbed into an empty well for safety.

For a long time she cowered at the foot of the well, terrified and weeping bitterly. At last she could bear it no longer, and scrambled into the open air. She found the house a heap of smouldering ruins, but she managed to pick out a few pots and pans, which she sold for money, and bought herself some men's clothes. Dressed as a boy

she went to the royal court and offered herself as a servant there. The king asked the young servant his name, and the reply came, 'Unfortunate.' The king liked the boy and immediately took him into his service; soon Unfortunate became his favourite of all the servants.

The prince was very sad when he heard that his sweetheart's house had been burnt to the ground, and concluded that Beauty had been burnt to death in the fire. The king believed it too, and ordered his son to woo and wed the daughter of a friendly neighbouring king.

The whole court and all the attendants set out for the wedding celebrations, and Beauty rode with them, her heart heavy with misery. She kept to the very rear of the procession, and sang in a clear melancholy voice:

> 'Beauty once was all my fame.
> Unfortunate is now my name.'

The prince heard her from a long way ahead. 'Who is that singing so beautifully?' he asked.

'It must be my page, Unfortunate,' replied the king. Once again the clear voice rang out:

> 'Beauty once was all my fame.
> Unfortunate is now my name.'

Once again the prince asked the king his father if it was really his page who was singing so beautifully, and the king replied that he was quite certain of it.

As the long procession drew near to the castle of the princess who was to be the prince's bride, the beautiful voice was heard yet again, clearer than ever:

> 'Beauty once was all my fame.
> Unfortunate is now my name.'

The prince wheeled his horse about, dug in his spurs and galloped to the end of the procession, and recognized Beauty at once, disguised as a page. He nodded to her joyfully, and then galloped back to the head of the procession, which was about to pass through the gate.

When all the guests were assembled in the great hall they were welcomed by the king and his daughter, the princess. 'Your Majesty,' said the prince to his future father-in-law, 'before I announce my solemn engagement to your daughter, I should like to ask you a simple question. I possess a beautiful chest, but some time ago I lost the key to it and so had to buy another. A short while later I found the old key. Tell me, Your Majesty, which key ought I to use?'

'Naturally you should use the old one,' replied the king. 'The old should always take precedence over the new.'

'That is just what I thought, Your Majesty,' replied the prince. 'So do not be angry with me if I cannot marry your daughter. For she is the new key, and there stands the old one.' And he took Beauty by the hand and led her to his father, saying, 'This is my bride, father.'

The old king was shocked and amazed. 'But that is Unfortunate, my page!' he cried. And many of the courtiers cried out, 'That is indeed Unfortunate.'

'No, father,' said the prince, 'it is by no means unfortunate. This is Beauty, my beloved bride.' And he took his leave from the gathered assembly, and led Beauty away with him to his most magnificent castle as his princess and his wife.

The House in the Forest

A poor woodcutter lived with his wife and three daughters in a little hut at the edge of a wild forest. One morning, as he was setting out to work, he said to his wife, 'Send our eldest daughter to me at midday with my lunch. I will take a bag of millet with me and strew it on the ground as I go, so that she will be able to find me easily.'

So when the sun stood high in the sky above the trees the girl set off with a bowl of soup. But the sparrows and larks, the blackbirds and finches, had long since pecked up the millet seed, so that the girl could not find her father. She wandered on in the hope of coming across him, until the sun sank and night fell over the forest. The leaves of the trees whispered in the darkness, the owls hooted and the girl became anxious and frightened.

Suddenly she saw a light twinkling through the trees, and hurried towards it, thinking that she would be able to find food and shelter for the night. She came to a little hut and knocked at the door, and a deep voice called, 'Come in!' So in she went. At a table sat an old man with a flowing white beard, which reached almost to the floor. Beside the stove sat three animals: a hen, a cock, and a brindled cow.

The girl explained to the old man that she had lost her way, and asked for a bed for the night.

The man said, 'Pretty hen, pretty cock, and you, my beautiful brindled cow, what do you think?'

'Dooks!' replied the animals, and that must have meant that she was welcome, for the old man said, 'Here you will find food and shelter. Go to the kitchen and cook our supper.'

In the kitchen the girl found plenty of everything and cooked a good meal, but she forgot about the three animals. She carried a huge steaming dish to the table, sat down beside the old man, and ate until she could eat no more. Then she said, 'I am tired. Have you a bed I can sleep in?'

The animals replied, 'You have eaten with our master, you have drunk with our master, but you have forgotten us. Now you shall see where you are to sleep!'

The old man said, 'Go upstairs and you will find a bedroom with two beds in it. There are clean sheets lying on them. Make both beds ready, and I will shortly come up to bed.'

So she climbed upstairs and made the beds and shook the pillows, and lay down to sleep without waiting to say good night to the old man. Soon afterwards he came upstairs, and when he saw that she was fast asleep he opened a trapdoor and let her down into the cellar.

Late that evening the woodcutter returned home, and reproached his wife for having forgotten his meal. 'But I didn't forget,' she replied. 'The girl set off with your soup, but she must have lost her way. I expect she will come back in the morning.'

Next day the woodcutter said, 'This time send our second daughter. I am taking a bag of lentils with me. Lentils are bigger than millet seeds, and will not get lost so easily. She will be able to see them clearly enough, and ought not to lose her way.'

So at midday the second daughter set out with a dish of stew, but the lentils had vanished, pecked up by all the birds of the forest. She lost her way amongst the trees, and when night fell she, too, saw the light flickering between the trees, and came to the little hut, where she asked for food and shelter. Once again the old man with the white beard asked, 'Pretty hen, pretty cock, and you, my beautiful brindled cow, what do you think?'

Again the animals replied, 'Dooks!' and everything happened exactly as on the previous day. The girl cooked a tasty meal, which she shared with the old man, but she forgot all about the animals; and when she asked where she was to sleep, the animals replied, 'You have eaten with our master, you have drunk with our master, but you have forgotten us. Now you shall see where you are to sleep!'

When she had fallen asleep, the old man came and looked at her, shook his head, and lowered her into the cellar.

On the third morning the woodcutter said to his wife, 'Today you must send our youngest daughter with my lunch. She has always been good and obedient, and is sure to find her way.'

But his wife hesitated, saying, 'Do you want me to lose my last darling daughter too?'

'Don't worry,' he replied. 'She is clever, and, in any case, this time I will strew peas as I go. They are much bigger than lentils, and should be quite easy to see.'

But when the third girl set out with her basket, the pigeons had eaten all the peas, and before long she was quite lost. As darkness fell, she, too, followed the light and knocked at the door of the little hut. She asked politely if she could by any chance have shelter for the night. The old man with the white beard turned to his animals, and asked, 'Pretty hen, pretty cock, and you, my beautiful brindled cow, what do you think?'

'Dooks!' they replied. The girl went to the hearth, where the animals lay, and stroked the hen and cock, and tickled the brindled cow between the horns. Then she cooked a fine soup, but as she set the soup bowls on the table she said, 'Are we to eat and leave the poor animals without anything?' And out she went to fetch corn for the cock and hen, and an armful of sweet-smelling hay for the cow.

'Eat well, dear animals,' she said. 'I'll fetch some fresh water for you in case you are thirsty.' She brought in a bucket of water and set it down before them. The cock and hen perched on the edge, dipped in their beaks and then tipped their heads right back in the way birds drink. When they had drunk, the brindled cow took a hearty draught.

When the animals had been fed the girl sat down at the

table with the old man, and ate what he had left. Before
long the cock and hen tucked their head under their wing,
and the brindled cow blinked her eyes sleepily. The girl
asked, 'Is it not our bed-time too?' And the old man said,
'Pretty hen, pretty cock, and you, my beautiful brindled
cow, what do you think?'

The animals replied, 'Dooks! You have eaten with us all,
you have drunk with us all, and you have shown us loving
care. We wish you a good night.'

The girl went upstairs, shook up the beds and spread
fresh linen sheets. When everything was ready, the old
man came and lay down in one of the beds, while she
climbed into the other. She said her prayers and was soon
fast asleep.

She slept soundly until midnight. But then there was such a commotion in the house that she woke up. There was a creaking and cracking in the corners, the door burst open and crashed back against the wall, the beams groaned, and the stairs seemed to be collapsing. Finally there was an ear-splitting crack, as though the roof were about to cave in. Then peace fell on the house, and the girl slept peacefully once more.

As the first rays of sunlight streamed into the room next morning the girl awoke – and what an extraordinary sight met her eyes! She found herself lying in a beautiful bed in the middle of a large room. At the windows hung golden curtains and on the walls tapestries of rich green silk, glowing with brightly coloured flowers. The bed was of ivory and the covers were of crimson velvet, and on a nearby stool lay a pair of slippers embroidered with pearls. She looked for the old man, but in his bed she saw a stranger – a handsome young man, who blinked his eyes and smiled at her as he awoke.

'I am a prince,' he said, 'and I was turned into the white-haired old man by a wicked witch. I was allowed to have no other company than my three faithul servants in the forms of a cock, a hen, and a brindled cow. Only a girl who showed herself kind and thoughtful towards animals as well as to men, could release me from the evil spell. You are the girl, and last night at midnight we became free. The little hut in the wood is once again my royal palace. And now, let us be married.'

The three servants were sent to fetch the girl's parents to the wedding. 'But where are my two sisters?' she asked, as they set out.

'They are locked in the cellar,' replied the prince. 'Tomorrow they will be taken into the forest, where they will have to work for a charcoal-burner until they have learnt to think of others, and not to let poor creatures starve.'

Snow-white

Once upon a time, in the middle of winter, when the snow-flakes were falling like feathers from the sky, a queen sat sewing at an open window, which had a frame of black ebony. As she sewed and watched the snow-flakes, the queen pricked her finger with the needle, and three drops of blood fell into the snow. The red looked so pretty in the white snow that she thought to herself how wonderful it would be if she could have a baby daughter as white as snow, as red as blood, and as black as the ebony of the frame.

Not long after, a baby daughter was born to her, whose skin was as white as snow, whose lips were as red as blood, and whose hair was as black as ebony, and the child was called Snow-white. But on the very day when Snow-white was born, the good queen died.

A year went by and the king took a new wife. She was a beautiful woman, but she was proud and haughty, and could not bear the thought of anyone being more beautiful than herself. She had a magic mirror, and whenever she looked into it she would say,

> 'Mirror, mirror, on the wall,
> Who is the fairest one of all?'

And the mirror would reply,

> 'Thou, Queen, art the fairest one of all.'

123

Then she was satisfied, for she knew that the mirror could speak only the truth.

The years passed, and with each day Snow-white grew more lovely. By the time she was seven years old she was as lovely as a spring morning and more beautiful by far than the queen. One day, the queen stepped up to her mirror and asked,

> 'Mirror, mirror, on the wall,
> Who is the fairest one of all?'

And the mirror replied,

> 'Thou, Queen, may'st fair and beauteous be,
> But Snow-white is lovelier far than thee.'

The queen started, and turned green and yellow with jealousy. From that moment, her heart turned with hatred whenever she saw Snow-white. Day by day her envy grew in her heart like weeds, until she had no peace. At last, she called a huntsman to her, and said, 'I cannot stand the sight of the child! Take her out into the wildest part of the forest and kill her, and bring me her heart and liver as proof of the deed.'

So the huntsman took the child out into the forest, but when he drew his long sharp hunting knife to kill Snow-white his heart melted, for she began to cry, saying, 'Spare my life, dear huntsman! I promise to run away into the forest and never come near the palace again.'

Because she was so pretty, and because he was not so cruel as the wicked queen, the huntsman had pity on her and said, 'Run away, then, poor child!' The wild beasts would soon catch her, he thought, yet he felt as though a great weight had been lifted from his heart because he would not have to kill her himself. Just then a young boar rushed out of the undergrowth. The huntsman caught it and cut out its heart and liver to take to the queen as proof.

Now Snow-white was all alone in the wild forest. She was so frightened that she began to run. She ran through thickets of prickly brambles and over sharp stones, and the wild beasts ran beside her but did no harm. She ran and ran until it began to grow dark. When she was almost exhausted she came to a little house in a clearing, and she went inside to rest.

The house was tiny, but everything in it was perfectly neat and tidy. There was a table with a snowy cloth, set with seven little plates, each with a little fork, spoon, and knife, and a little wine-glass arranged round it. Along the wall stood seven little beds, with snow-white linen sheets and fleecy blankets.

Snow-white was so hungry and thirsty that she ate a piece of bread and a spoonful of vegetables from each of the seven plates, and drank a sip of wine from each of the glasses, for she did not want to take everything from one plate. She was so tired that she lay down in one of the little beds, but it was too short. The next one was too long, and she tried them all until she came to the last one, which was just right; and there she said her prayers and was soon fast asleep.

When darkness fell the owners of the little house came home. They were seven dwarfs, who spent their day digging in the mountains for gold and iron. When they had lit their seven little lamps and the room was bright and cheerful, they saw that things were not quite as tidy as they had left them.

The first dwarf said, 'Who has been sitting on my chair?'
The second said, 'Who has been eating from my plate?'
The third, 'Who has been nibbling my bread?'
The fourth, 'Who has tasted my vegetables?'
The fifth, 'Who has been using my fork?'
The sixth, 'Who has been cutting with my knife?'
The seventh, 'Who has been drinking from my glass?'

Then the first dwarf looked round and saw that his bed-clothes were slightly ruffled. 'Who has been lying in my bed?' he asked. The others looked at their beds, and said, 'Someone has been lying in my bed too!' But the seventh dwarf saw Snow-white lying asleep in his bed, and called to the others to come and see. They came running up, holding their lanterns high in order to see Snow-white better. Their eyes opened wide with astonishment, for they had never before seen such a lovely girl. 'What a beautiful child!' they cried in delight, and they tiptoed quietly away, being careful not to waken her.

Then the dwarfs went to sleep in their own beds, ex-

cept the seventh, who spent one hour in each of the other six beds.

Snow-white awoke next morning, and was startled to see the seven dwarfs, but they spoke kindly to her, and asked her name.

'My name is Snow-white,' she replied.

'How did you come here?' they asked. So she told them how the wicked queen had tried to kill her, how the huntsman had spared her life, and how she had run all day through the forest until she had arrived exhausted at their little house.

'Will you keep house for us?' they asked. 'Will you cook, and make our beds for us, wash, sew, and darn for us, and will you keep everything neat and tidy? If you will, you can stay here, and you shall have everything you want.'

'Of course,' replied Snow-white, 'I should like nothing better.' So she stayed with the dwarfs, and kept house for them.

Every morning the dwarfs set out for the mountains to dig for iron and gold, and every evening Snow-white had supper ready for them on their return. All day long she was alone, and the kind dwarfs warned her not to let any stranger into the cottage. 'Beware of the wicked queen!' they said. 'It will not be long before she finds out where you are.'

The queen, however, was certain that now she was the most beautiful woman in all the land. She went up to the mirror, and said,

> 'Mirror, mirror, on the wall,
> Who is the fairest one of all?'

But the mirror answered,

> 'Thou, Queen, may'st fair and beauteous be,
> But over the hills in a woodland glade
> Where seven dwarfs their home have made
> Snow-white is lovelier far than thee.'

The queen was full of rage, for she knew that the mirror could speak only the truth. She knew now that the hunts-man had deceived her, and that Snow-white was still alive. She thought and thought how she could kill her, for envy would allow her no rest until she was once again the most beautiful woman in all the land. At last her plan was ready. She dyed her face and disguised herself as an old pedlar-woman, so that no one could recognise her. In this guise she travelled to the dwarfs' cottage, knocked at the door, and called, 'Pretty things for sale. Pretty things for sale.'

Snow-white peeped out of the window. 'What do you have in the basket?' she asked.

'Hundreds of pretty things,' replied the old pedlar-

128

woman. 'Ribbons and laces in various colours.' And she pulled out a lace of pure silk.

Surely there can be no harm in letting the woman in, thought Snow-white, as she unbolted the door, for she wanted to buy the pretty lace.

'Come,' said the old woman. 'Let me lace your bodice properly for you.'

Snow-white had no suspicions, and allowed her to lace up her bodice. But the old woman pulled the lace so tight that Snow-white was unable to breathe and fell to the floor in a dead faint.

'Now you are no longer the fairest in the land,' exulted the wicked queen, as she hurried away from the dwarfs' cottage.

Not long afterwards the seven dwarfs returned home from a hard day's work in the mountains, and they were horrified to find their dear Snow-white lying on the floor. She seemed to be dead, for she made no movement, but when the dwarfs lifted her up they soon saw what was the matter, and quickly cut the lace. Immediately Snow-white began to breathe again, and the colour returned to her cheeks.

When the dwarfs heard what had happened, they said, 'The old pedlar-woman was most certainly the wicked queen. You must be careful, and on no account must you let anyone into the house when we are away.'

Meanwhile the queen had returned to the palace, where she went without delay to her mirror and asked,

'Mirror, mirror on the wall,
Who is the fairest one of all?'

And the mirror replied as before,

'Thou, Queen, may'st fair and beauteous be,
    But over the hills in a woodland glade
    Where seven dwarfs their home have made
    Snow-white is lovelier far than thee.'

When the queen heard this she was angrier than ever, for she knew that Snow-white must still be alive. 'Now I must think of something,' she said to herself, 'that will be sure to kill her properly.' And with the black arts of witch-craft, which she understood, she made a beautiful but poisoned comb. Then she disguised herself as another old woman, crossed the hills to the cottage of the seven dwarfs, and knocked at the door, crying, 'Pretty things for sale! Very cheap!'

Snow-white looked out of the window, and said, 'Please don't stop here – I am not allowed to let anyone in.'

'Surely you are allowed to *look* at my things,' said the old woman, holding up the comb. Snow-white liked it so much that she forgot the dwarfs' instructions and opened the door. They had no sooner agreed on the price than the old woman said, 'Now let me comb your beautiful hair.' Snow-white suspected nothing, but immediately the comb touched her hair the powerful poison began to work, and she fell to the floor in a dead faint.

'That's an end to you now, my beauty!' said the wicked queen, as she slammed the door and hurried away.

But luckily it was late evening and the seven dwarfs soon arrived home, to find Snow-white lying on the floor. They suspected the wicked queen immediately, and soon found the comb entangled in her hair. They pulled it out, and before long Snow-white recovered consciousness and told them what had happened. Once again they warned her to be careful and to let no one into the house.

Meanwhile the queen, back in her palace, asked her mirror,

> 'Mirror, mirror, on the wall,
> Who is the fairest one of all?'

And the mirror again replied,

> 'Thou, Queen, may'st fair and beauteous be,
> But over the hills in a woodland glade
> Where seven dwarfs their home have made
> Snow-white is lovelier far than thee.'

At this the wicked queen's fury knew no bounds. 'Snow-white must die, at all costs!' she declared. She wasted no time, but locked herself in a secret chamber where no one ever came, and prepared a poisoned apple. Everyone who saw the apple would long to taste it, for it was bright red on one side and a delicate pale yellow on the other. But the tiniest bite would bring death.

When the apple was ready, the queen disguised herself as an old peasant woman with a wrinkled brown face, and crossed the mountains to the cottage of the seven dwarfs, deep in the forest. As soon as she knocked on the door, Snow-white looked out of the window, saying, 'I cannot let anyone into the house – the seven dwarfs have forbidden me to.'

'Never you mind,' said the old woman. 'All I want is to give you an apple.'

'Oh no!' said Snow-white. 'They told me I was not to accept anything.'

'Are you afraid of poison?' asked the old woman. 'Look, I'll cut the apple in two halves. I'll eat the yellow half, and you eat the red half.' For the apple was so skilfully made that all the poison was in the red half, while the yellow half was quite safe.

Snow-white longed for a bite of the apple, and when she saw the old peasant-woman eating half of it she reached out her hand and took the poisoned half; but she had no more than bitten it when she fell down dead.

The wicked queen shrieked with wild laughter when she saw Snow-white lying lifeless on the ground! 'White as snow, red as blood, and black as ebony!' she cried. 'This time not all the dwarfs in the world will be able to waken you!'

When she arrived home again she went straight to her mirror.

> 'Mirror, mirror, on the wall,
> Who is the fairest one of all?'

And at last the mirror replied,

> 'Thou, Queen, art the fairest one of all.'

The queen's envious heart was satisfied at last, for she knew that the mirror could speak only the truth.

When the dwarfs arrived home that evening they found Snow-white lying on the ground. Not the slightest breath came from her lips, for she was quite dead. They lifted her up and searched for any sign of poison, they combed her hair and loosened her clothes, they washed her in water and wine, but all in vain.

The seven dwarfs laid her on a bier and knelt beside it, weeping, for seven long days. They thought they ought to bury her, but she still looked as fresh and bright as when she had been alive, and her cheeks were as rosy as ever. 'We can never bury such a beautiful creature in the black earth!' they said. So, carefully and laboriously, they prepared for her a beautiful crystal casket, in which she could be seen from all sides, and on top they wrote her name and her royal title in gold letters. Then they carried the casket to the top of a nearby hill, where one of them sat and watched over her night and day.

Even the animals and birds came and wept for Snow-white, and delicate little butterflies gently fanned the casket with their wings. She lay there for a long, long time, but did not moulder away. She looked as though she were simply sleeping, for she was still as white as snow, as red as blood, and as black as ebony.

Now it happened one day that a king's son came riding through the wood. He trotted up to the dwarfs' cottage to ask for shelter for the night. He saw the crystal casket on the hill and read the golden letters. 'Let me have the casket,' he entreated the dwarfs. 'I will let you have anything you want for it!'

'No,' said the dwarfs. 'We will not part with our Snow-white for all the gold in the whole world.'

'Then *give* her to me,' said the prince, 'for I cannot live without her. I will cherish her as the dearest thing in the world.'

The good dwarfs were so moved by his words that they gave him the casket. The prince ordered two stalwart servants to lift it on to their shoulders, but one of them tripped over a root and stumbled, jerking the precious load and dislodging the piece of poisoned apple from Snow-white's throat. Her eyes flickered and opened, and she looked about her in wonder. She pushed open the lid of the casket, and sprang lightly to the ground as if nothing had ever been the matter. 'Where am I?' she asked. 'Have I been sleeping?'

The prince was overjoyed, and explained everything to
her. 'Come with me to my father's palace,' he begged. 'I
love you more dearly than anything else in the whole
world, and I want you to be my bride.'

Snow-white fell in love with the prince, and went with
him to his father's palace, where a magnificent wedding
was held. All the important people in the land and the
neighbouring kingdoms were invited, including the vain
and wicked queen. In her castle far away she put on her
finest clothes for the wedding feast, and stepped before
her mirror, saying,

'Mirror, mirror, on the wall,
Who is the fairest one of all?'

And the mirror answered,

> 'Thou, Queen, may'st fair and beauteous be,
> But the young queen is lovelier far than thee.'

At first the wicked queen was angry, but then she grew frightened, so frightened that she did not know which way to turn. She knew that she should not go to the wedding for fear of her life, but she felt that she had to see the young queen. When she entered the banqueting hall she recognized Snow-white immediately, and stood rooted to the spot with fear and terror. But red-hot iron slippers were set in front of her, and she had to put them on and dance until she fell to the ground – dead.

Cinderella

A rich man's wife was very ill. As she felt her end approaching, she called her only daughter to her bedside and said, 'Dear child, God will look after you as long as you are good and kind, and I shall always be with you.' With these words she closed her eyes and died.

Each day the girl went and wept at her mother's grave, and she was always good and kind to every living creature. Winter came, covering the grave with a white mantle of snow, and when the spring sunshine lifted it again the girl's father married another wife. The new wife had two daughters of her own, who were beautiful to look at, but cold-hearted and selfish.

So began a time of misery for the poor step-daughter, for they took all her fine clothes away from her, and gave her wooden clogs and a ragged grey skirt. From morning till night she worked about the house, sweeping and dusting, cooking and washing. Her step-sisters played all sorts of spiteful tricks on her, and teased her continually. They would scatter lentils in the ashes of the fire, and would make her sit in the hearth until she had picked them all out again. At night, when she was worn out and exhausted, she was not allowed to sleep in a cosy bed, but had to lie down by the kitchen fire among the ashes and the cinders. And that is how they came to call her Cinderella.

One day her father was setting out to visit a nearby fair, and asked the girls what they would like him to bring them.

'Fine clothes,' replied one of the step-daughters without

hesitation. 'Pearls and precious stones,' replied the other.

'And you, Cinderella, what would you like?' he asked.

'Just bring me the first twig that touches your hat on the way back,' she replied.

So he bought fine clothes and pearls and precious stones for the two step-daughters, and for Cinderella he picked a green hazel twig which had brushed his hat from his head on the way home. On his return he gave his step-daughters their gifts, and to Cinderella he gave the hazel twig.

Cinderella thanked him, and went to her mother's grave, where she planted the twig. As she did so the tears fell from her eyes and watered the ground; and the twig sprouted and grew into a fine tree. Three times a day Cinderella went to weep and pray at the grave. Each time a little white bird would come and perch on the hazel tree, and if she wished for anything, he would throw it down to her.

The time came when the king announced that a ball was to be held at the palace. It would last for three days, and all the young ladies of the land were invited, for the prince was to choose a bride. The two step-sisters were delighted, and called Cinderella to them. 'Come and polish our shoes!' they cried. 'We are going to the ball at the royal palace.'

Cinderella did as she was told, but she was sad because she would have liked to go to the ball. She plucked up courage and asked her step-mother if she could go.

'You?' she said scornfully. 'You are covered with dust and ashes, how can *you* go to the palace?' But Cinderella persisted, and at last her step-mother said, 'I will empty a bag of lentils into the ashes. If you can pick them all out within two hours you may come to the ball.'

Cinderella hurried to the kitchen door and called up to the birds in the trees surrounding the garden, 'Come, all you birds. Come and help me to pick up lentils.'

At once two white pigeons flew down, closely followed by two turtledoves, and with a great whirring of wings flocks of birds came fluttering into the kitchen. They began to peck away at the ashes, nodding their little heads up and down and dropping the lentils into a bowl, and in less than an hour they had finished. Cinderella took the bowl to her step-mother, sure that she would now be allowed to go to the ball.

'Oh no!' said the step-mother. 'You have neither a dress nor dancing shoes. Everyone would laugh at you!' But when Cinderella cried more than ever, she said, 'Very well. If you can pick *two* bowls of lentils out of the ashes in less than one hour, you may go to the ball. And that, she thought to herself, will be quite impossible. But as soon as she had gone Cinderella opened the kitchen door, and cried, 'Come, all you birds. Come and help me to pick up lentils.'

Down flew the two white pigeons, followed by the two turtle-doves, and with a whirring of wings flocks of birds again came crowding into the kitchen. Peck, peck, peck, they went, dropping the lentils one by one into the two basins, and in less than half an hour the task was finished.

Cinderella was overjoyed, but, when she came with the two bowls of lentils, her step-mother simply repeated that she could not go. 'Do you want to make us a laughing-stock?' she asked, and turning on her heel, off she went to the ball with her two proud daughters.

Cinderella was bitterly disappointed, but instead of vainly weeping she went straight to her mother's grave, and called,

'Shiver and shake, my little tree,
Throw gold and silver over me!'

Immediately the little white bird threw down a beautiful dress of silk. that shimmered now gold now silver, and a pair of delicate slippers, embroidered with gold and silver threads. She thanked the bird as she put on the dress and slippers, and hurried to the palace.

As Cinderella came into the ballroom, all eyes turned to gaze at her beauty. The prince himself crossed the room to welcome her, and led her into the dancing. All evening he would dance with no one else, and if any other young man came to take her away, he said, 'No, she is my partner.'

They danced until it was very late, and Cinderella was anxious to leave for home. 'I will come with you,' said the prince, for he wanted to find out where his beautiful partner lived. But she slipped away from him in the dark, and hid in the dove-cot in her father's garden. The prince waited until Cinderella's father came home, and told him that the strange girl was hiding in the dove-cot. The father wondered whether it might be Cinderella, and fetched an axe to open up the dove-cot. But there was no one inside, for Cinderella had slipped quietly away to the hazel tree, where she had left her fine dress and slippers with the little white bird.

By the time the prince and her father came into the house, Cinderella, dressed once more in her dirty rags, was lying among the ashes of the kitchen fire.

Next day, when her step-mother and step-sisters set off for the palace, Cinderella went again to the hazel tree and said,

'Shiver and shake, my little tree,
Throw gold and silver over me!'

The bird threw down an even more magnificent dress than before, and everyone at the palace was amazed at Cinderella's beauty.

The prince had waited for her to come, and at once led her into the ballroom, and danced with her alone. If anyone else asked her to dance, he said, 'No, she is my partner.'

When it grew late Cinderella took her leave, and set off for home. The prince tried to follow her, but she slipped away from him and ran into the garden behind her home. As nimbly as a squirrel she climbed up a tall pear tree laden with fine, ripe pears. The prince did not know where to look for her, but soon her father appeared, and the prince said, 'The strange girl has given me the slip. I think she must be hiding in this pear tree.'

Her father wondered whether it might be Cinderella, and fetched an axe to cut down the tree. But there was no one in the branches. When they went into the kitchen they found Cinderella lying among the ashes and the cinders as before. She had jumped down from the pear tree, and had changed back into her old grey skirt, leaving her beautiful clothes with the white bird in the hazel tree.

On the third day, after her step-mother and step-sisters had left for the ball, Cinderella went again to her mother's grave and said to the hazel tree,

'Shiver and shake, my little tree,
Throw gold and silver over me!'

This time the white bird threw over her a dress which was the most beautiful he had yet given her, and slippers of beaten gold. All the guests at the palace were more amazed than ever when they saw her. Once again the prince would dance with no one else, and would not part with her to any other dancer, saying, 'She is my partner.'

When it grew late and Cinderella wanted to go home, the prince went with her, but she ran so fast that he could not keep up with her. This time, however, the prince had been clever. He had painted the palace steps with pitch,

and when Cinderella ran down them the slipper from her left foot stuck fast and was left behind. The prince picked it up and examined it. It was neat and dainty, and made of the purest beaten gold. Next morning he went to Cinderella's father, and said, 'I will marry the girl whose foot this golden slipper fits.'

The step-sisters were delighted to hear this, for they both had beautiful feet. The elder sister went into her room to try on the shoe, while her mother stood by. But her big toe would not fit inside, for the shoe was too small. Her mother handed her a knife, saying, 'Cut off your toe! Once you are queen you will no longer need to walk.'

So the girl cut off her big toe and forced her foot into the shoe. In spite of the pain, she smiled brightly and went to the prince, who lifted her on to his horse, and rode away with her to make her his bride. As they passed by the grave, however, two white doves, who were sitting in the hazel tree, called out,

'Look around, do!
There's blood on the shoe!
The shoe is too tight.
It cannot be right!'

The prince looked down, and saw blood welling out of the shoe. So he took the false bride back to the house, saying that a mistake had been made, and that the other sister should try the shoe.

So the younger sister went into her room to try on the shoe. Her toes fitted in perfectly, but her heel simply would not go in. 'Never mind!' said her mother, handing her the knife. 'Cut off your heel! Once you are queen you will never need to walk.'

So the girl cut a piece from her heel, and forced her foot into the shoe. In spite of the pain, she smiled brightly and went to the prince, who lifted her on to his horse, and rode away with her to make her his bride. As they passed under the hazel tree, however, the two white doves cooed,

'Look around, do!
There's blood on the shoe!
The shoe is too tight.
It cannot be right.'

The prince looked down and saw blood trickling from the shoe and staining her white stockings. He took the false bride home again and said, 'I was mistaken. Have you another daughter?'

'No,' said the man. 'Only the scruffy little daughter of my first wife, but she cannot possibly be your bride.' The prince insisted that they should call her, but the stepmother objected, saying, 'Oh no, she is far too dirty to show herself here!' The prince refused to change his mind, and at last Cinderella was called.

She washed her hands and face, and went and curtsied before the prince, who handed her the golden slipper. She drew her dainty little foot out of its heavy wooden clog, and put on the slipper with ease. It was a perfect fit. As she smiled up at him, the prince recognized her as his beautiful dancing-partner. 'This is indeed my bride!' he cried.

The step-sisters and step-mother were pale with rage and envy as the prince lifted Cinderella on to his horse, and rode away with her.

As the couple rode past the hazel tree, the two white doves cooed,

> 'Look around, do!
> No blood on the shoe!
> Her stocking is white.
> The shoe is just right.'

With these words the doves flew down on to Cinderella's shoulders, one perching on the right shoulder, and the other on the left. And there they remained.

On the wedding day the two treacherous step-sisters were full of flattering words, for they wanted to share in the good fortune. On the way to the ceremony the elder sister walked on the right of the bridal pair, and the younger sister on the left. But the two white doves pecked out one eye from each of them, and on the way back from the church, when the elder sister was on the left and the younger on the right, the white doves pecked out their remaining eyes. In this way they were punished with blindness for the rest of their lives for all their cruelty and unkindness.

Lucky Hans

Hans had served his master for seven long years. 'My time is up now,' he said to his master. 'Give me my wages, for I want to go home to my mother.'

'You have served me well and faithfully,' replied his master. 'Your reward shall be as good as your service.' With these words he gave Hans a huge lump of gold as big as his head. Hans pulled his handkerchief out of his pocket, wrapped up the lump of gold, lifted it on to his shoulder, and set out for home.

The way was long and exhausting, and his eyes lit up when he suddenly saw a man on horseback, trotting merrily along at ease with the world. 'How wonderful it must be to ride!' he exclaimed. 'There you sit, just as if you were in an armchair. You don't stub your toes against stones, you save your shoe leather, and you cover the ground at a fine rate.'

The horseman heard his words, and pulled up. 'Hullo, Hans!' he called. 'If that's what you think, why are you walking?'

'I have to,' Hans explained sadly. 'I have this heavy old lump to carry around with me. It is pure gold, it's true, but it is so heavy that I cannot stand upright.'

'I know,' said the horseman. 'Let us make an exchange. I will give you my horse, and you give me your lump.'

'Delighted!' cried Hans. 'But I must warn you that you will soon be tired out with carrying it.'

So the horseman dismounted and took Hans's bundle. He helped Hans up on to the horse, and put the reins in his

146

hands. 'If you want it to go faster,' he explained, 'you simply click your tongue and say, "Hup! Hup!" '

Hans was very pleased with himself as he sat on the horse's back and rode along without having to exert himself at all. After a while he thought he would like to go faster, so he clicked his tongue and cried, 'Hup! Hup!' At once the horse broke into a brisk canter, and before Hans knew what was happening he flew over the horse's head and landed in a muddy ditch. The horse would have run away, had it not been caught by a farmer who was passing by, driving a cow before him. After making sure that no bones were broken, Hans stood up and said sulkily, 'A fine game, this riding. when the horse does its best to break your neck! That's the last time you'll ever catch *me* riding a horse!'

'Well,' said the farmer, 'if it suits you, I shall be pleased to exchange my cow for your horse.' Hans agreed gladly, and the farmer leapt into the saddle and rode off.

Hans drove the cow quietly along, and thought how lucky he had been. As long as I have bread, he said to himself, I can have bread with butter and cheese on it as often as I want! If I am thirsty, all I have to do is to milk the cow. What else could I possibly ask for?

When he came to a wayside inn he halted and ate all the food he had with him, and bought a small glass of beer for a few pence. Then he drove his cow on towards his mother's village.

As midday approached the heat became more and more oppressive, and Hans found himself crossing a wide heath. He grew so hot and thirsty that he stopped to milk the cow in order to quench his thirst. He tethered her to a tree-trunk, and, as he had no bucket, he laid his leather cap on the ground beneath her. But, no matter how hard he tried, not a single drop of milk appeared. He was so clumsy that the poor beast lost patience with him, and gave him a powerful kick on the head with her hind leg, which sent him sprawling on the ground.

For a few moments Hans did not know where he was, but luckily for him a butcher chanced to pass that way, pushing before him a young pig in a wheelbarrow. 'What's the trouble, Hans?' he called. Hans told him what had happened, and the butcher gave him a drink from his water-bottle. 'That cow will never give you much milk,' he said. 'She is far too old, and is fit only for ploughing or for meat.'

'Who would have thought it?' said Hans, rubbing his head. 'I suppose I could use her for meat – but I don't like beef! It is too dry for me. But, a young pig like yours, that would taste fine – and you could have sausages, too.'

'Listen, Hans,' said the butcher. 'If you like, I will help you by exchanging my little pig for your old cow.'

'Many thanks indeed for your generosity,' cried Hans, and he handed over his cow, leading the pig away in exchange.

He continued on his way, well contented with his lot. Whenever anything happened to annoy him, something always turned up to put matters right. Before long he met a young fellow who was carrying a plump goose under his arm. Hans told him all about his good fortune, and how he had made so many favourable exchanges. The young fellow told him that he was taking the goose to a christening feast. 'Just feel how heavy it is!' he said, holding it up by the wings. 'I've been fattening it for eight weeks. It will make a tasty roast.'

'Yes,' said Hans, weighing the goose in his hands. 'It's quite heavy. But so is my pig.'

Meanwhile the young fellow was looking about suspiciously and shaking his head doubtfully at the pig. 'You know,' he said, 'the mayor of our village has just had a pig stolen, and I'm afraid – I'm very much afraid – that it's the one you have here. He has sent people out to look for it, and it would be a sad thing for you if you were caught. They would certainly lock you up in the dungeon.'

Poor Hans was scared out of his wits. 'What can I do?' he cried. 'Would you exchange your goose for my pig?'

'Well,' said the lad, 'it's a little risky, but I hate to think of you getting into trouble.' So he set the goose down, seized the pig, and made off quickly down another track.

Freed of his worries, Hans took the goose under his arm and plodded on towards his mother's cottage. 'Another good exchange!' he said to himself. 'I shall have a wonderful roast and plenty of goose dripping for my bread for several months, and I shall have all the beautiful soft feathers besides. I think I will make a pillow with the feathers, so that I shall be able to sleep comfortably at nights. How pleased my mother will be!'

As he walked through the last village on his way home, he came across a grinder with his grindstone on a barrow. As he turned the grindstone, the grinder sang,

'I sharpen scissors and knives all day.
My stone drives all the rust away.'

Hans paused to watch him at work. 'You seem to have a very happy job.'

'Yes indeed,' replied the grinder. 'This trade is a great money-spinner. A good grinder will find money whenever

he puts his hand in his pocket. But where did you buy that fine goose?'

'I didn't buy it,' said Hans, 'I exchanged my pig for it.'

'And your pig?'

'Oh, I was given that in exchange for my cow.'

'And the cow?'

'I was given that in exchange for my horse.'

'And the horse?'

'I changed my lump of gold for that – a lump as big as my head.'

'And the gold?'

'That was my wages for seven years' service.'

'You seem to have done very well for yourself,' said the grinder. 'How would you like to hear the money jingle in your pocket every time you stand up or sit down?'

'How could I do that?' asked Hans.

'By becoming a grinder, like me. All you need is a grind-stone – the rest is easy. You could have mine, if you like. It is a little worn, so I will let you have it in exchange for your goose, if you like.'

'Will you really?' said Hans. 'I am the luckiest person in the whole world. What shall I have to worry about, if I have money whenever I put my hand in my pocket?' So he handed over his goose, and took the grindstone.

'And here,' said the grinder, as he picked up a heavy boulder from the roadside, 'is another useful stone, which you can use for hammering straight all your bent nails. Take this too, and look after it well!'

Hans picked up his two stones, and went happily on his way. His eyes sparkled with joy. 'I must have been born under a lucky star,' he said. 'Everything I could possibly wish for seems to come true!'

He had been on his feet all day, and by this time he was tired. He was also beginning to feel very hungry, for he had eaten all his food in his joy at having the cow. Soon he was stumbling along a few yards at a time, pausing every few minutes to rest. His two stones weighed him down painfully, and he thought how good it would be if only he did not have to carry them. He crawled at a snail's pace to a spring by the side of the track, to take another rest and refresh himself with a drink of cool water. He laid his stones carefully by the edge of the spring so that they would not be damaged as he sat down, and then he bent to drink. But as he stretched he knocked against the stones, and they fell into the spring with a great splash.

When he had watched them sink right to the bottom, Hans jumped for joy, and then knelt with tears in his eyes to thank God for delivering him from his troublesome burden, which was all that had prevented him from being perfectly happy.

'There's no one under the sun as lucky as I,' he cried. With a light heart, and free of every burden, he ran lightly on his way and was soon home in his mother's cottage.

Good Luck and Bad Luck

On a rocky crag in the foothills of a great mountain range there was once a village which looked just like a stork's nest on a tower. In this village lived two men, one of whom had Good Luck for his guardian, while the other had Bad Luck for his. The first man was called Mr Well-done, and the second Mr Ill-done.

Mr Well-done began by selling linen and silks from a barrow in the streets; then he opened a shop; and, because Good Luck was his guardian, he very soon became the richest man in the village. He was well liked by everyone, for money did not spoil him.

In Mr Ill-done's house, on the other hand, there was neither flour nor bread; only hunger, poverty, and crying children.

Now one day Mr Well-done sent for Mr Ill-done, who came humbly to the door. 'God bless Your Excellency!' he said.

'God be kind to you, my friend!' replied Mr Well-done. 'But why are you looking so miserable?'

'Everything you set your hand to seems to prosper,' said Mr Ill-done, 'whereas I am the target of every ill wind of fortune.'

'My friend,' said Mr Well-done, 'in this world there have always been people who laugh and people who cry. But let us get down to business. I have sent for you because I want you to go to the palace of my guardian, Good Luck, and tell her from me that I am quite satisfied with what she has done for me, and that I want nothing more. I will give you two hundred silver pieces to pay for the journey.'

Instead of jumping for joy at this generous offer and seizing the opportunity without delay, Mr Ill-done was filled with greed. 'What!' he exclaimed. 'Good Luck's palace is miles away, right up in the mountains. It will take me ages to find a way through all the thorns and thickets to reach it. I'll do it only if you pay me three hundred.'

This seemed shamelessly greedy to Mr Well-done, but he made no objections. As he was leaving, Mr Ill-done was again overcome by greed. He turned and said that a mere three hundred silver pieces was after all very little to pay for the job.

'Will you go for a hundred and fifty?' asked Mr Well-done, who by this time was thoroughly annoyed.

'You must be joking! If I won't go for three hundred, am I likely to go for a hundred and fifty?'

'Then don't go at all,' said Mr Well-done.

This reply disconcerted Mr Ill-done, who had been expecting a higher offer. But he needed the money so badly that he turned and said he would go for a hundred and fifty.

'Will you go for a hundred?' asked Mr Well-done.

'This is not the way to do business,' said Mr Ill-done. 'No, I will *not* go for a hundred.'

'Then don't go at all,' said Mr Well-done.

Mr Ill-done stamped out of the room, but as soon as he

was in the street he realized how stupid he had been. He kicked himself for not accepting the offer of three hundred, and went back to Mr Well-done. 'Mr Well-done,' he said, 'I'll go for a hundred.'

'Will you go for fifty?' asked the rich man.

'Am I to wear away my shoe leather for the sake of a miserable fifty?' exclaimed Mr Ill-done. 'Good-day to you, Mr Well-done!'

'Until we meet again, my friend.'

Once again, he no sooner found himself in the street than he realized how foolish he had been to refuse fifty silver pieces, when he did not possess a penny. 'Your Excellency,' he cried as he hurried back, 'I'll go for fifty!'

'Will you go for ten?' asked the rich man.

'Of course I will!' cried Mr Ill-done before the other could change his mind and make a lower offer.

For a whole day he climbed upwards over boulder-strewn hillsides and through deep ravines, until he came to a rocky pinnacle which was so steep that a goat could hardly have found a way up. At the very top of this pinnacle stood Good Luck's marble palace with doors of gold.

When Mr Ill-done had at last scrambled to the top and entered the magnificent palace, he called for Good Luck. A beautiful woman appeared, dressed in magnificent robes and jewels.

'What do you want?' she asked.

'Mr Well-done has sent me to tell you that he is quite satisfied with what he has, and wants nothing more.'

'Tell him,' replied the beautiful woman, 'that I shall give him what I want to give him, whether he wants it or not. Off you go, for you are infecting my palace with the stench of poverty.'

'Haven't you some small thing for me?' asked Mr Ill-done.

'I am not your guardian. I can do nothing for you,' replied the woman. 'Your guardian lives at the back of my palace. Go and ask *her* to help you.' And with these words she whirled away, singing like a canary.

Mr Ill-done crept round to the back of the palace, where he found his own guardian's dwelling. It was a heap of stones, black and desolate, and in every cranny there lived a viper or some other monster. 'So this is where my guardian lives!' he exclaimed. 'I may as well see her ugly face while I am here.' And he called for her. At the first shout a miserable old hag came crawling out of the rubble. Her eyes were bleary and had no lashes, and her wrinkled mouth had not a single tooth.

'What do you want with me?' she screeched, in a voice which rasped like two rusty scythes being scraped together.

'To send you to the devil, where you belong!' he replied.

'Have a care,' warned the old hag. 'You have earned

your ten silver pieces only because I was asleep. If I had been awake, I should have seen to it that you did not get so much as a brass farthing for your journey.'

The Magic Table, the Gold-donkey, and the Cudgel in the Sack

A long time ago there lived a tailor who had three sons and a nanny-goat. The goat kept them all supplied with her milk, so it was of great importance to see that she was well fed, and the three sons took it in turn to lead her out to pasture.

One day the eldest son took her to the churchyard, where some of the juiciest plants were to be found, and there he let her play and eat as much as she wanted. In the evening, when it was time to go home, he asked. 'Goat, have you had enough?' And the goat answered,

> 'I've eaten so well,
> I'm beginning to swell, meh! meh!'

'Come away home then,' said the young fellow, and he led her home and tied her up in the stable.

'Well?' said the old tailor, 'did you give the goat plenty to eat?'

'Of course, father,' he replied. 'She has eaten so well she's beginning to swell.'

The tailor wanted to make quite sure, so he went down to the stable and asked the goat, 'Did you have plenty to eat?' And the goat replied,

'There was not a blade of grass
     In the narrow stony pass.
  I shall starve to death, alas, meh! meh!'

'The good-for-nothing!' cried the tailor. 'Fancy leaving such a fine animal to starve!' And he seized his measuring-rod and drove the lad out of the house.

Next day it was the second son's turn. He took the goat to a special place beside the garden hedge where the grass was particularly long and juicy, and the goat spent the whole day busily eating. In the evening, when it was time to go home, he asked, 'Goat, have you had enough?' And the goat answered,

'I've eaten so well,
     I'm beginning to swell, meh! meh!'

'Come away home then,' said the young fellow, and he led her home to the stable and tied her up.

'Well?' said the tailor. 'Did you give the goat plenty to eat?'

'Oh yes, father,' he replied. 'She has eaten so well she's beginning to swell.'

The tailor wanted to be certain that the goat was satisfied, so he went to the stable and asked her, 'Did you have plenty to eat today?'

'There was not a blade of grass
     In the narrow stony pass,
  I shall starve to death, alas, meh! meh!'

'What's this?' cried the old tailor, and ran upstairs for his measuring-rod. 'What a liar you are!' he shouted at his son. 'You told me the goat was well fed, and she is starving! Leave my house at once!' And he drove him out with the measuring-rod.

Now it was the third son's turn, and – to make quite sure that all was well – he sought out the most luscious grass that could be found anywhere, and the goat ate without stopping from morning till evening. When it was time to go home, he asked, 'Goat, have you had enough?' And the goat replied,

> 'I've eaten so well,
> I'm beginning to swell, meh! meh!'

'Come away home then,' said the lad, and he tied her up in the stable.

'Well?' said the old tailor. 'Has the goat had plenty to eat?'

'Yes, indeed, Father. She has eaten so well she's beginning to swell.'

The tailor was not convinced, so he went down and asked, 'Goat, did you have plenty to eat?' And the wicked goat replied,

> 'There was not a blade of grass
> In the narrow stony pass,
> I shall starve to death, alas, meh! meh!'

'What a brood of liars!' exclaimed the tailor. 'Each as mischievous and undutiful as the other!' He rushed upstairs and beat the boy so severely with the measuring-rod that he fled from the house as fast as his legs would carry him.

Now the old tailor was alone with the goat. Next morning he went down to the stable and patted her, saying, 'Come, my dear. Today I will take you to pasture myself.'

He led her to the hedges where the grass grew greenest, and where there were plenty of all the plants and herbs that goats like best. 'Here you can eat to your heart's content,' he said. When it began to grow dark, he asked her, 'Goat, have you had enough?' And she replied,

> 'I've eaten so well,
> I'm beginning to swell.'

'Come away home then,' said the tailor, and he took her and tied her up in the stable. 'Are you satisfied at last?' he asked. But the goat replied, just as she had done before,

> 'There was not a blade of grass
> In the narrow stony pass,
> I shall starve to death, alas, meh! meh!'

When the tailor heard these words, he saw that the goat had made a fool of him, and that he had driven away his three sons without cause. 'You ungrateful creature!' he cried. 'Before I send you away I will make you ashamed to show yourself amongst honest people!' And he seized a shaving-brush, soap, and razor, lathered the goat's head and neck, and shaved her until she was as bald as your hand. Then he fetched his whip, and sent her bounding away with the first few strokes.

The tailor was lonely now, and in his sadness he wished his sons would come home again; but no one knew where they had gone.

In the meantime the eldest boy had apprenticed himself to a carpenter. He learnt quickly and well, and worked hard. When his time was up and he wanted to set out on his travels, his master gave him a little table. It was nothing much to look at – just an ordinary wooden table. But it

was special all the same, for if anyone set it down and
said, 'Table, lay yourself!' it was immediately covered
with a fine linen tablecloth, and laden with as many steaming dishes of roast meats and other fine things as there was
room for, together with a fine big glass of claret.

'There's enough food and drink here for the whole of my
life,' thought the young fellow. He travelled for some
time, never bothering whether the inns were good or bad,
for he always had plenty to eat and drink. If there was no
inn to be found, he simply set down the table in a wood
or in the fields, and said, 'Table, lay yourself!' – and immediately there was a steaming meal in front of him.

At last he thought he should return to his father, whose
anger would by this time have abated. Now it came about
that on the way home he had to spend a night at an inn
which was already full when he arrived. The other visitors

asked him to join them, or else, they said, he would find difficulty in obtaining a meal.

'No, thank you,' replied the carpenter. 'I would rather that you were *my* guests.'

They thought he was joking, but he set down his table in the middle of the room and said, 'Table, lay yourself!' At once it was covered with all sorts of food, far better than the landlord could have provided.

'Fall to, my friends,' he said. The visitors were all amazed, but fell to with a will, and ate as much as they could stuff into themselves. What surprised them most of all was the way the dishes filled themselves up again as soon as they were emptied.

Meanwhile the innkeeper was watching from a corner. He could not understand how the table worked, but he saw immediately how valuable it would be to him in running his inn.

The carpenter and his friends made merry until late that night, but at last the young fellow went upstairs and set his little table on the floor beside his bed. By this time the innkeeper had remembered that he had a similar table lying in his attic, and he crept into the carpenter's room in the middle of the night to exchange his old table for the magic one.

Next morning the carpenter paid his bill, took his table (not realizing that there was anything wrong with it) and went on his way. He reached home at midday and was received with open arms by his father.

'Well, my boy,' said the old man, 'what have you learnt?'

'I have become a carpenter, Father.'

'An honourable trade,' replied the old man. 'Have you brought anything back from your travels?'

'This table is my most valuable possession, Father.'

The old tailor examined it from all angles. 'But this is hardly a masterpiece!' he exclaimed. 'It is just a very ordinary old table. I could do better myself!'

'No, Father, this is no ordinary table. If I put it down and tell it to lay itself, it is immediately covered with the most tasty dishes and as much of the finest wine as you can drink. Invite all your friends and relations to dinner, and you will see how well they can dine from my table!'

So a large company was gathered together, and when they were all ready he put his table down in the middle of the room, and said, 'Table, lay yourself!' Nothing happened. The table was as empty as any other table. The poor fellow saw that his table had been changed, and he had been made to look a perfect fool in front of all these people. All his relations and his father's friends laughed at him, and they had to go home hungry.

Once again the old man took up his needle and thread and carried on with his tailoring, while his son went to work for a master-carpenter.

The second son had apprenticed himself to a miller, and when his time was up his master said to him, 'You have been a good boy and have worked well, so I am giving you a very special kind of donkey as a farewell gift. He cannot pull a cart, nor can he carry sacks.'

'What use is he, then?' asked the lad.

'He coughs up gold,' replied the miller. 'If you make him stand on a cloth, and say "Bricklebrit" to him, he will cough up as many gold coins as you want.'

The lad thanked the miller for this marvellous present, and went out into the world. Whenever he needed money, he just said, 'Bricklebrit', and it rained gold coins, and all he had to do was to pick them up. In all his travels he bought the best of everything, for he always had more money than he knew what to do with.

After he had wandered round the world for some time he felt a longing to see his father again. He felt sure the old tailor would give him a welcome, if only for the sake of his wonderful donkey. Now it happened that he stopped for the night at the same inn where his brother's table had been changed. The innkeeper was going to take his donkey to the stable for him, but the young fellow said, 'Don't bother! I always prefer to tie him up myself, so that I know where he is.'

This seemed strange to the innkeeper, and he thought his guest must be a penniless vagabond. So when the lad pulled out two gold coins and called for the most expensive food and wine the innkeeper's eyes popped with surprise.

After dinner the young fellow asked if he owed any more money. The innkeeper, who was a miserly fellow, asked him for a few more gold coins. The young man felt in his pocket, but there was no money left. 'Wait a moment,' he said. 'I will go and fetch some money.' But he took the tablecloth with him.

The innkeeper's curiosity knew no bounds, and when his guest had bolted the stable door from the inside the innkeeper peeped through a knot-hole to see what was going on. The stranger spread the cloth under the donkey, and said, 'Bricklebrit,' and immediately the animal began to cough up gold, so much gold that it rained down on to the cloth.

The innkeeper could not believe his eyes. 'I could do with a money-box like that!' he said.

His guest paid his bill and went up to bed. During the night, however, the innkeeper crept into the stable and took away the gold-donkey, leaving an ordinary donkey in its place.

Next morning the young fellow led the donkey out of the stable and set off for home, arriving there at midday.

His father was delighted to see him. 'What have you been doing all this time, my boy?' he asked.

'I have learnt a miller's trade, Father,' the lad replied.

'Have you brought anything back from your travels?'

'Only a donkey.'

'But we have plenty of donkeys here,' said his father. 'I would rather have had a good goat.'

'I know,' replied his son. 'But this is no ordinary donkey. When I say "Bricklebrit" to him he coughs up a whole sheetful of gold pieces. Just send for all our relations, and I will make them rich.'

'That would suit me very well,' said the old man. 'I could give up tailoring.' Off he went at once and fetched all the relations. As soon as they came the young miller spread out a cloth and led the donkey into the room. 'Now watch!' he said, and cried 'Bricklebrit!' But not a single gold piece did the donkey cough up. It was quite plain that the poor creature did not understand the art of producing gold. Not every donkey is clever enough for that. The poor lad saw that he had been robbed, and apologised to all his relations for sending them home as poor as they had come. The old man had to start sewing again, and his son took work with a miller.

The third brother apprenticed himself to a turner. This is highly skilled work and it took the longest to learn. While he was still apprenticed his brothers told him in a letter how the wicked innkeeper had robbed them of their most valuable possessions. When his time was up, his master presented him with a sack, saying, 'There's a cudgel in it.'

'The sack will be useful,' said the apprentice, 'but why should I carry around this heavy cudgel? It makes the sack so heavy.'

'I will tell you why,' said the master. 'If anyone does you an injury all you need do is to say, "Out of the sack, cudgel!" – and it will leap out of the sack and beat your enemies mercilessly until you say, "Into the sack, cudgel!"'

The young fellow thanked him, and went on his way. If anyone tried to attack him he said, 'Out of the sack, cudgel!' – and immediately the cudgel would leap out of the sack and beat his assailants without mercy.

One evening he arrived at the inn where his two brothers had been robbed. He laid his sack on the table before him, and began to talk of all the wonderful things he had seen in the world. 'Yes,' he said, 'magic tables and golden donkeys and such-like things are two a penny! Quite useful things, if you happen to possess them, but nothing in comparison with the treasure I have in this sack.'

The innkeeper pricked up his ears. What in the world could it be? He thought the sack must be filled with jewels and precious stones, and determined to add it to his treasures.

So in the middle of the night, when his guest appeared to be sound asleep, the innkeeper crept into his room and found the sack beneath his pillow. He pulled at it cautiously; and that was what the young fellow had been waiting for. When the innkeeper at last gave the sack an impatient tug, he cried, 'Out of the sack, cudgel!' At once the cudgel leapt out of the sack and gave the innkeeper a sound beating, until he fell to the ground black and blue all over. The innkeeper cried out for mercy, but the louder he cried the faster the cudgel rained blows upon him.

At last the young turner ordered the cudgel back into the sack. 'It will start again,' he said, 'unless you give me the magic table and the gold-donkey which you stole from my brothers.'

'I promise!' gasped the exhausted innkeeper. 'Only keep that devilish thing in the sack!'

Next morning the lad set out for home, with the table and donkey as well as his cudgel and sack. His father was glad to see him, and asked him what trade he had learnt during his long absence from home.

'I am a turner, Father,' he replied.

'A good trade,' said his father 'Have you brought anything back with you?'

'A wonderful thing, Father. A cudgel in a sack.'

'Why on earth did you bother with that? You can cut a cudgel from a tree any day!'

'Not one like this, Father. Whenever I say, "Out of the sack, cudgel!" – it leaps out and gives all my enemies a sound thrashing. With the help of this cudgel I have reclaimed the magic table and gold-donkey, which a rogue of an innkeeper stole from my brothers. Call them both now, and invite all our relations to dine and to fill their pockets with gold.'

The old tailor was not very hopeful, but he called all his relations. The turner spread a cloth on the ground, and led in the donkey. 'Now, dear brother,' he said, 'speak to him!'

The miller said, 'Bricklebrit,' and immediately gold coins poured down on the cloth until there were more than all the people could possibly carry away. (I am sure you would have liked to be there!)

The turner then fetched the little table from the kitchen, and said, 'Well, brother, speak to it!' And scarcely had the carpenter said, 'Table, lay yourself!' than the table was laden with steaming dishes of food. Never had such a sumptuous banquet been seen!

When the guests had left, the old tailor threw away his needles and thread, his scissors and his measuring-rod, and settled down to live in peace and luxury with his three sons.

Witzenspitzel

There was once a king of Roundabout-Hereabouts. Amongst his many servants he had a page called Witzenspitzel, who was so clever that the king was always showering him with presents. The other pages and servants at the court were all jealous of Witzenspitzel, for, while he was rewarded for his cleverness, they were always being punished for their stupidity.

You can understand, therefore, how angry the servants were with Witzenspitzel, and how they muttered and grumbled day after day, wondering how they could make him lose favour with the king. One of them strewed peas round the throne, in the hope that Witzenspitzel would stumble and smash the glass sceptre when the king handed it to him. Another stuck melon pips on the soles of his shoes in the hope that he would slip and spill the soup over the king's robes. A third servant blew midges through a straw into the king's hair while Witzenspitzel was brushing it. But all their efforts were in vain, for Witzenspitzel saw through their tricks, and obeyed the king's commands without mishap.

When all their plots had miscarried, the servants hit upon another idea. The king had an enemy who was a constant thorn in the flesh to him. This was the Giant Longjaw, who lived with his wife Fatface in a splendid castle on a crag in the middle of a dense forest. No other creature would live there, apart from Scared-of-hens his lion, Honeybeard his bear, Lamb-chaser his wolf, and Hare-catcher his dog. These were his only servants, and he used them to torment the folk of Roundabout-Hereabouts. He also had a horse in his stable, called Swift-as-the-wind, and on this horse he escaped from anyone who pursued him.

Now there lived next to the kingdom of Roundabout-Hereabouts a very rich widow called Mistress Speedy, who possessed a great many fields and orchards, plantations and farmhouses, and had a daughter called Nimble. The king of Roundabouts-Hereabouts was very eager to join all the neighbouring estates to his kingdom, and he was an ardent suitor for Mistress Speedy's hand. She, however, would take for her husband only a man who could travel extremely fast, so she arranged a race to the church, in which the competitors could use any means of transport they pleased. Whoever arrived first would be rewarded by her hand in marriage, together with all her land.

The king of Roundabout-Hereabouts called all his servants to him, and asked for suggestions. 'How can I be the first at the church and so win Mistress Speedy's hand?'

'That's easy,' replied his servants. 'You must ride to the church on Swift-as-the-wind, Giant Longjaw's horse. No creature can move faster than Swft-as-the-wind. Send Witzenspitzel to fetch him. He will be able to overcome all difficulties.'

But the wicked servants really hoped that Giant Longjaw would kill Witzenspitzel – indeed, they had little doubt that this would be the outcome.

So the king ordered Witzenspitzel to fetch the horse. The cunning fellow knew all about Giant Longjaw's strange household, so he brought out a wheelbarrow and set a beehive on top of it. Then he fetched a sack, in which he put a hen, a hare, and a lamb, and laid it in the barrow

169

with the beehive. He took a length of string and a large box of snuff, and finally he fixed a strong pair of spurs to his boots, and off he set with his barrow.

Towards evening he reached the top of the crag, and saw the giant's castle through the trees. He waited until it was quite dark and everyone was asleep. Giant Longjaw and Fatface his wife, Scared-of-hens his lion, Honeybeard his bear, Lamb-chaser his wolf and Hare-catcher his dog were all snoring so loudly that the whole castle shook. Only the horse, Swift-as-the-wind, seemed to be awake, for he was pawing the ground restlessly in his stable.

Quietly, quietly, Witzenspitzel tied his long string between two trees right in front of the castle gates, just a foot above the ground, and laid his box of snuff in the middle of the track. Then he set his beehive at the foot of a tree beside the track, and at last he was ready to untie Swift-as-the-wind. Quickly he leapt on to the horse's back, with the sack containing the cock, the hare, and the lamb slung over his shoulders, and dug his spurs into the horse's sides so that it shot from the stable. But Swift-as-the-wind could speak, and called, 'Longjaw and Fatface! Honeybeard and Scared-of-hens! Lamb-chaser and Hare-catcher! Witzenspitzel is riding me away!'

Longjaw and Fatface awoke with a start when they heard Swift-as-the-wind's cry for help, and immediately wakened Honeybeard the bear, Scared-of-hens the lion, Lamb-chaser the wolf, and Hare-catcher the dog. They all rushed out of the castle together to catch Witzenspitzel, but the giant and his wife tripped over the string across the gate and fell flat on their faces, with their eyes and their noses buried in the big box of snuff. They rubbed their eyes until the tears streamed down their faces, and sneezed again and again, until at last Longjaw managed to sit up and say, 'Bless you, Fatface!'

'Thank you,' she replied. 'And bless you too, Longjaw!'

'Thank you,' said Longjaw, and by the time they had rubbed all the snuff out of their eyes, and sneezed it all out of their noses, Witzenspitzel was far away.

Honeybeard the bear was the next out of the castle gates, but when he reached the beehive he stopped and put his paw inside to see if there was any honey. Out swarmed the bees, and stung him so violently that he fled back into the castle, roaring, and slammed the door behind him.

By this time Witzenspitzel had reached the foot of the crag, and he was almost out of the wood when he heard Scared-of-hens the lion close at his heels. Quick as lightning he took the hen out of his sack. It flew to the top of a high tree where it began to cackle noisily. Nothing terrified the lion more than a hen's cackling, so he turned tail and fled back to the castle.

Before long Witzenspitzel heard Lamb-chaser the wolf pounding along behind him, so he took the lamb out of his sack. At once the wolf raced off in pursuit of the lamb, and Witzenspitzel galloped on.

He was already within sight of the city when he heard a loud barking behind him. He looked over his shoulder to see Hare-catcher the dog close on the horse's heels. Quickly he let the hare out of the sack, and Hare-catcher turned to chase it, leaving Witzenspitzel to reach the city in safety, without any further trouble.

The king was full of gratitude to Witzenspitzel for bringing him the horse, but the treacherous servants were furious that he had returned unharmed. Next morning the king won the race on Swift-as-the-wind without the slightest difficulty, and his marriage to Mistress Speedy took place immediately.

While he was taking his queen back to his castle, the servants said to him, 'It must indeed be wonderful to have Giant Longjaw's horse, but would it not be even better to have back all the magnificent robes and other booty which he has stolen from your kingdom during the past few years? That would be a fine gift for your queen! Witzenspitzel is clever – he will bring them back if you order him to do so.'

The king was easily persuaded, and gave Witzenspitzel his orders that very evening. The other servants were delighted, convinced that he would not escape from the giant's clutches a second time.

All that Witzenspitzel took with him this time was a good strong sack and some rope. He reached Longjaw's castle just as night was falling, and sat down on a tree-stump to wait until everyone was asleep. When he thought it was safe he crept forward towards the gate, but hardly had he begun to wriggle through it when he heard Fatface cry, 'My pillow is too low, Longjaw. Fetch me a bundle of straw.'

Quick as a thought Witzenspitzel slipped into the straw, and Longjaw lifted him with the straw and laid him in the bed, under the pillow.

As soon as the giant and his wife were both sound asleep, Witzenspitzel stretched out his hand and gave Giant Longjaw's hair a vicious tug. Then he did the same to Fatface. In a flash they were awake and hitting each other, each of them thinking that it was the other's fault. While they were still fighting Witzenspitzel crept out of the straw and hid behind the bed.

He waited for them to go to sleep again before he crept out. Quietly he bundled together all the finest robes he could find, stuffed them into his sack, and tied it gently but firmly to the tail of Scared-of-hens the lion without waking him. Then he tied Honeybeard the bear, Lamb-chaser the wolf, and Hare-catcher the dog – who were all sound asleep on the floor – to the giants' bed. He opened the door wide, so that a howling draught whistled through the room, and pulled the cover and blankets off the bed. He wrapped himself quickly in the bedcover, and sat on

top of the sackful of clothes which he had tied to the tail of the sleeping lion.

It was not long before Fatface awoke and felt the cold wind blowing round her legs. She shook Longjaw by the shoulder, saying, 'Give me back the blankets! I have nothing over me at all!'

Longjaw woke up freezing, and said, 'Nonsense! You have taken the bedclothes from me!' They began to quarrel, and Witzenspitzel started to laugh loudly. The two giants realized then that something was wrong. 'Stop thief!' they cried. 'Up, Scared-of-hens! Up, Lamb-chaser! Up, Honeybeard! Up, Hare-catcher!'

The animals all leapt to their feet, and the lion shot

through the doorway, pulling Witzenspitzel and the sack of clothes like a carriage behind him. 'Cluck, cluck, chook, chook, chook!' cried Witzenspitzel. This frightened poor Scared-of-hens out of his wits, and he ran faster and faster. When they arrived at the city gates, Witzenspitzel cut the rope round the lion's tail, and the beast ran so violently into the gates that he fell down dead.

Meanwhile the other animals had tried to pursue Witzenspitzel, but they were tied to the bed, which stuck in the doorway, for it was far too big to pass through. They dragged the bed round and round the room, so that Longjaw and Fatface fell out on to the floor. Longjaw was so angry that he struck the poor animals dead in a fit of temper.

The king was delighted at the beautiful robes Witzenspitzel had brought him, for never had anyone seen such magnificent garments. There was a hunting-suit made out

of the skins of all the animals in the world, beautifully sewn together. There was another suit made of the feathers of all the birds of the air, and yet another made of the scales of all the fishes of the sea. Fatface's gardening-dress was quite extraordinary, composed of all sorts of flowers and vegetables and fruits. But best of all was the bedcover, which was of the skins of thousands of bats, sewn carefully together and adorned with thousands of precious stones, which sparkled like the stars of the Milky Way.

The king and queen were overjoyed, and rewarded Witzenspitzel handsomely, but the other servants were furious that he had not been caught and killed by Giant Longjaw.

One day, not long after this, they put it into the king's head that all he lacked was the giant's castle. So the king sent for Witzenspitzel, and said, 'Capture Longjaw's castle for me, and I shall see that you are well rewarded.'

Witzenspitzel was in no way dismayed, and soon he stood once again before the castle gates. The giant was not at home, but he found Fatface busy chopping wood, with the sweat pouring down her face in streams.

'Good day to you!' said Witzenspitzel. 'Why are you doing all this hard work? Do you not have any servants?'

'My husband has gone to invite our cousins to a feast,' replied Fatface. 'But I have to do all the cooking and preparations myself, for my husband killed the bear and the dog and the wolf who used to help us, and the lion has not come back yet.'

'That is hard luck!' said Witzenspitzel. 'But I shall be glad to help you. Off you go to meet your dear husband, and leave me to get on with the work here.'

Fatface accepted this offer gladly, and set out to meet her husband. As soon as she was out of sight Witzenspitzel set to work to dig an enormous deep hole immediately outside the castle gates. When it was deep enough he covered it so carefully with branches and leaves and grass that no one could have guessed there was a hole. Then he lit candles and lamps in all the banqueting halls of the castle, beat on a huge jelly-pan with the soup-ladle, blew loudly on a long hunting-horn, and cried at the top of his voice, 'Long Live the King of Roundabout-Hereabouts!'

When Longjaw and Fatface drew near the castle they heard the sound of celebrations and saw the bright light streaming from the windows. They were furious, and ran full tilt towards the gates. Crash! – they fell into the hole which Witzenspitzel had dug, and all the shouting in the world could not help them.

Witzenspitzel took the giant's keys to the king, who set out at once for the castle with his wife and Nimble, his daughter-in-law. Witzenspitzel took them on a tour of the whole castle, and it took them fourteen days to visit every banqueting-hall, bedroom, cellar, kitchen, laundry, scullery, pantry, and attic. When the inspection was completed, the king asked Witzenspitzel to choose his reward. He thought for a moment, and said, 'Give me Nimble as my bride, and Longjaw and Fatface as my housekeepers.'

And so it came about. After a splendid wedding, Witzenspitzel and Nimble lived in the giants' castle, and prospered greatly. But the other servants turned green with envy and, no matter how hard they scrubbed, their faces remained green to the end of their days.

The Flying Trunk

There was once a merchant who was so rich that he could have paved the whole street with gold – and the alleyways too – without noticing the cost. But he did no such thing, for he knew how to look after his money. If he invested a penny, he expected to earn half a crown in return.

The day came, however, when this rich merchant died. All his money was inherited by his only son, who spent all his time amusing himself. He would make paper dragons out of notes and he would use gold coins for skimming on the lake, instead of flat stones. In this way he soon exhausted his great wealth and before long only a few pence remained of his whole inheritance, and all he had left of his magnificent clothes was a threadbare old dressing-gown and a worn-out pair of slippers.

His friends thought it no more than he deserved and avoided him if they met him in the street. Only one of them felt sorry for him, and gave him an old trunk, telling him to say the words, 'Pack up,' to it. That was very kind of the friend, but the young man had nothing left to pack ! So he put himself in the trunk.

It was, however, a magic trunk, and would fly through the air as soon as its lock was pressed. As the young man pressed the lock, the trunk shot like an arrow up the chimney and into the clouds. It flew on and on, but it creaked so alarmingly that the young man was afraid it would fall to pieces.

At last the trunk came down in the land of the Turks. The young man hid the trunk under some leaves in a wood, and walked into the city. No one questioned him, for the Turks wore the same sort of clothes as he was wearing – a dressing-gown and slippers. He met a woman with a little boy, and said, 'Tell me – what is that high tower over there, and why are all the windows so high up?'

'That is where the sultan's daughter lives,' she replied. 'It was foretold that a young man would bring her great unhappiness, so no one is allowed to go near her except the sultan and his wife.'

'Thank you,' said the young man. He went back to the wood where he had hidden his magic trunk, flew in it up to the roof of the princess's tower, and crept through the window into her room.

She looked so lovely as she lay sleeping that he had to kiss her. She awoke with a start, but he explained that he was a god, who had flown through the air specially to see her, and she was very pleased.

He sat down beside her and put his arm round her waist, and began to tell her the most wonderful story about her eyes – how they were like deep lagoons, with all her thoughts swimming about in them like mermaids. Then he told her stories about her lips and her forehead – never had she heard such entrancing stories!

Finally he asked her to marry him, and after a moment's consideration she said she would. 'But you must come again on Saturday,' she said, 'when my parents come to take tea with me. They will be very proud to hear that I am to marry a god! But be ready to tell a good story, for my mother likes a good moral tale, and my father likes a story which will make him laugh.'

'Very well,' he said, 'I will bring you a pretty tale as a

wedding gift.' As he was about to depart, the princess gave him a sword studded with gold coins, which were just what he needed!

Off he flew and bought himself a fine new silk dressing-gown, and then he sat down in the wood to compose a suitable story. It had to be ready by Saturday, and that was not easy. By the time he put the finishing touches to it it was Saturday afternoon.

The sultan and his wife and the entire court were there with the princess, and he was graciously received.

'Will you tell us a story?' asked the sultan's wife. 'One that is profound and edifying.'

'Certainly,' replied the young man. 'I shall be glad to.' And this is the story he told. Pay attention!

'There were once some matches, who were very proud of their ancestry. They had come from a great old pine tree in the forest, and they were all a tiny part of this tree. They lay now on a mantelpiece between an old iron pot and a tinder-box and told nostalgic tales of their childhood.

' "Oh yes," they said, "those were wonderful times when we were still part of the green branch. Every morning we had dew-drops for breakfast, and all day long we basked in the sun (except when it was raining), and all the little birds used to come and tell us stories. We knew how well off we were, for the other trees round about had only summer clothes, whereas we wore our lovely green clothes all the year round, summer and winter. The day came, however, when the woodmen came amongst us, and in a single day our whole family was felled. Our main trunk was taken to be the mast of a beautiful new ship that was to sail right round the world; and we, the branches, have the honourable task of providing the world with light and heat."

' "I have quite a different song to sing," said the iron pot, who lay beside the matches. "Ever since I saw the light of day I have been scoured and scrubbed many thousands of times, and I have cooked many thousands of meals. I am the most important piece of furniture in the house, and it is my greatest joy to sit on the shelf, clean and spotless after meals, and chat with my comrades."

' "Let's not waste so much time talking!" exclaimed the tinder-box, striking the steel against its flint to make the sparks fly. "Let's have a jolly evening!"

' "Yes," said the matches. "Let's decide which of us is the most important."

' "Oh no," objected the iron pot. "I don't like talking

181

about myself in that way. Let each of us tell the tale of his life instead. I will begin. I was born on the Danish coast . . ."

' "A superb beginning!" cried all the plates in unison. "Everybody will love this story!"

' "I spent my youth there in a quiet family. The furniture was polished, the floor waxed, and we had fresh curtains every fortnight."

' "What a good story!" exclaimed the broom. "It is quite clear that you know a lot about housekeeping."

' "Yes, that is obvious," said the bucket, giving a little leap that splashed some of its water on to the floor.

'The iron pot continued his story, and the end was as good as the beginning. The plates all clattered with joy, and the broom swept up some parsley from the garden and crowned the iron pot with it, partly because he knew it would annoy the others, and partly because he wanted the pot to crown him on the following day.

' "Now I am going to dance," said the pair of tongs, and began to twirl and kick her legs so high that the old chair burst its seams in surprise. "Can I have a crown too?" pleaded the tongs, panting.

'The teapot was asked to sing, but excused herself on the grounds that she could sing only when she was hot. This was sheer affectation, however, for she preferred to sing only at tea-time in her mistress's drawing-room.

'On the window ledge lay an old pen, which the maid used for writing her messages. She was a very ordinary old pen, and had become badly stained through being dipped too deep into the ink-pot. "Let's not bother about the teapot and her sulky airs!" she declared. "If she won't sing, let her keep quiet. There's a nightingale in the birdcage who can sing the most beautiful melodies, even though she has never been taught."

' "I consider it most unseemly," said the tea-kettle, who was a half-sister to the teapot, "that a strange bird should be given a hearing in this company. I call upon the basket to give judgment in this matter!"

' "You good-for-nothing crowd!" exclaimed the basket. "Is this a profitable way to spend an evening? Would it not be much more sensible to put everything in the house in order, tidily? Everything ought to be in its proper place. I will draw up a list of instructions."

' "Let's bustle about!" they all cried together.

'At that moment the door opened, and in came the maid. Immediately they all stood still, and no one dared to budge. The maid took the matches and struck a light, and what a marvellous spluttering and glow of flame there was!

'Now everyone can see, thought the matches, that we are the most beautiful and most useful things in the house. How light and bright we are! But almost at once they had burnt out and died!'

'That was a wonderful story!' said the sultan's wife. 'I felt I was lying right beside the matches on the mantel-piece. Yes, you must marry our daughter.'

'I agree,' said the sultan. 'The wedding will take place next Monday.'

The whole city was brightly lit on the evening before the wedding. Bread and twisty rolls were distributed to the population, and urchins thronged the lanes and public streets, whistling and shouting. It was a magnificent occasion.

The young bridegroom thought he should make a small

contribution to the festivities, so he bought rockets and all sorts of fireworks, which he took up with him in his magic trunk. They cracked and exploded and showered down bright sparks. The Turks had never seen such a marvellous sight.

When the young man had landed his magic trunk in the wood once more, he hid it carefully and set off on foot into town, to ask the people how his display had looked from below. They all had something different to say to him about it. Everyone seemed to have seen something which the others had not, but his show had undoubtedly made a great impression on them all.

'He is clearly a very powerful god!' said one. 'His eyes flashed like stars, and his beard was like a waterfall,' said another. 'He flew in a fiery cloak,' said a third, 'and pretty angel-faces peered out from the folds.'

It was surprising to hear all these strange tales about himself. And to think that he was to be married to the most beautiful girl on the very next day!

He returned to the wood, intending to lie down and rest in his magic trunk – but where was it? It was no-where to be seen! Oh, horror – it had been burnt. A spark from one of the fireworks must have set it alight, and now there was nothing left but a tiny heap of ashes. Now he could no longer fly through the air, no longer reach his bride.

All day long the princess waited at the top of her tower for her bridegroom. Perhaps she is waiting there still.

And he? He roams the world and tells stories. But they are no longer as light-hearted as the tale of the matches.

The Six who Went Together through the World

There was once a very talented man who had served his king faithfully and bravely in the wars. When the war was over, however, he was dismissed from the army, and received three pence to cover his expenses. 'This tiny sum is of no use to me!' he exclaimed angrily. 'If only I can find the right people to help me I may yet force the king to give me the treasures of the entire kingdom.'

Angrily he wandered off into the forest, where he met a man who had pulled up six tall trees by the roots, as if they had been blades of corn. 'Will you be my servant,' he asked, 'and come with me?'

'Yes, I will,' replied the man. 'But let me first take home this little bundle of twigs to my mother.'

He took one of the trees and wrapped it round the other five, lifted the bundle on to his shoulder and carried it away. Before long he returned to follow his master, who said, 'We two should get on well together.'

After they had travelled some distance they came across a huntsman kneeling on one knee, who was holding a rifle at his shoulder and taking aim. 'What are you shooting, my friend?' asked the master.

'Two miles from here there is a fly sitting on the branch of an oak tree,' he said. 'I am trying to shoot out its left eye.'

'Come with me then,' said the master. 'We three should do well together in the world.'

The huntsman was ready to accompany them, and

before long they came to seven windmills whose sails were whirling merrily round although there was not a breath of wind, and not a leaf was stirring on the trees. 'I wonder what is driving those windmills?' said the man. 'I cannot feel any wind.' And he went on his way with his servants.

Two miles further on they found a man sitting on a fallen tree-trunk, who was holding one nostril and blowing through the other. 'What are you doing?' they asked.

'Two miles from here are seven windmills,' he replied. 'I am blowing the sails round.'

'Come with me then,' said the master. 'We four ought to do well together in the world.'

The blower climbed down from his tree-trunk, and went with them. They had not gone far before they met a man standing on one leg, whose other leg had been unbuckled and was lying on the ground beside him. 'That is a strange way to rest,' said the master.

'I am a runner,' replied the man. 'I have to unbuckle one of my legs to prevent myself from going too fast. If I wear both my legs, I run faster than any bird can fly.'

'Come with me then,' said the master. 'We five should do well together in the world.'

On they went, and before long they met a man wearing a cap pulled right down over one ear. 'Don't play the fool!' said the master. 'Put your cap on straight, man!'

'Oh no, I can't do that,' replied the man. 'If I do, there will be a hard frost, and all the birds will fall dead from the sky.'

'Come with me then,' said the master. 'We six should do well together in the world.'

Soon they came to a city where the king had made it known that whoever ran a race against his daughter and won could marry the girl, but that if he lost the race he must lose his head also. The master entered for the race, but told the king that his servant would run in his place. 'Very well,' said the king, 'but your servant's life and your own must both be at stake.'

The agreement was settled, and the runner strapped on his second leg. 'Run quickly, and win the race for us!' said the master. The two competitors were to fetch a jugful of water from a distant well. The princess and the runner were given their jugs, and the race began, but by the time the princess had taken her first stride there was no sign of the runner.

In no time he had reached the well, filled his jug, and turned round for the return journey. Half-way back, however, he began to feel tired. He lay down and fell asleep, setting the jug on the ground beside him. He used a horse's skull which he found lying nearby as a pillow, so that he would not be too comfortable or oversleep.

Meantime the princess, who was an excellent runner, had filled her jug at the well and was on the way back. When she saw her opponent lying asleep she stopped and emptied his jug before running on.

The race would surely have been lost had not the sharp-eyed huntsman seen from the castle ramparts what had happened. He loaded his rifle, took careful aim, and shot the horse's skull from under the runner's head without touching him. The runner leapt to his feet, and saw at once that his jug was empty. He raced back to the well, filled the jug to the brim, and flashed past the princess, to reach the finishing-post long before her. 'I really had to run that time!' he exclaimed.

The king and his daughter were not pleased to think that

the princess would have to marry a common soldier, so they considered carefully how they might get rid of him and his companions. 'I think I know a way,' said the king at last. And he called the six men, saying, 'You must be hungry after your travels. I have prepared a good, hearty meal for you.'

He led them into a room whose floor, walls, and doors were all made of solid iron, and whose windows were barred with the strongest steel. In the middle of the floor was a table groaning beneath the weight of a sumptuous banquet, and the men sat down to eat. As he left them, the king had the door locked and bolted from the outside, and ordered the cook to light an immense fire in the room below, until the iron floor became red-hot.

The cook piled more and more fuel on to the fire below, and the six comrades sitting round the table began to feel a trifle warm. To begin with they did not think very much about it, but soon the heat became quite intolerable and they tried to open the door – only to find that it was locked. They tried the windows, but they too were shut fast, and the six realized that the king was trying to burn them alive.

'He won't get away with this!' exclaimed the fellow with the cap. 'I will bring on a frost, and send the flames quivering back into the ashes.' So he put his cap straight on his head, and immediately there fell such a frost that the food began to freeze on the plates.

After a few hours the king thought the six comrades must surely be burnt to cinders, and had the door opened. He was surprised to find them safe and sound, and even more surprised to see that they were shivering. They asked politely whether they could come out and warm themselves, for it was so cold in the room that all the food had frozen solid.

The king was furious and went down to scold the cook for disobeying orders. But the cook pointed indignantly to the fierce, leaping flames, which were greedily licking the iron floor of the room above.

The king realized at once that he was not going to rid himself of the six comrades easily So he called the master, and said, 'Will you accept gold instead of my daughter? If so, you may have as much as you want.'

'Most certainly,' replied the master. 'If you will give me as much gold as my servant can carry, I will gladly renounce my claim to your daughter. I will come back in a fortnight to collect it.'

The king sighed with relief, and the master departed with his five comrades. He called together all the tailors in the entire kingdom, and they sat together day and night for a fortnight, sewing the most enormous sack that had ever been seen. When it was ready, the strong fellow who could uproot trees returned to the king, with the sack slung over his shoulder.

'What a powerful-looking fellow!' exclaimed the king. He hardly dared to think how much gold such a man would be able to carry away, but he called on sixteen of his strongest men to bring a ton of gold. The strong tree-lifter lifted it all in one hand and flung it into his enormous sack. 'Why have you brought so little?' he asked. 'This hardly fills the bottom!'

Bit by bit the king had to send for all the gold in his entire kingdom. The strong fellow threw it all into his sack, but it was still barely half full. 'Bring more!' he cried. 'These few scraps are of no use to anyone.' Seven

thousand wagons full of gold were gathered together, and
the strong fellow threw them all into his sack, gold and
wagons and oxen and all. 'I suppose this will have to do,'
he sighed, as he tied up the sack. 'If I wait for the sack to
be filled I shall be here for ever!' He heaved the sack up
on his shoulders, and returned to his master and comrades.

The king's fury knew no bounds when he saw one man
carrying off the entire wealth of his kingdom. He called up
his cavalry and sent them after the six, to bring them back
to him, dead or alive, together with the sack of gold. Two
regiments of horsemen soon found the six, and shouted,
'You are prisoners! Lay down the gold, or you will be
hacked into little pieces!'

'What's that!' exclaimed the windmill-blower. 'Prisoners, are we? I'll see you all dancing in mid-air first!' He
held one nostril and blew through the other, and the

hundreds of men of the two regiments went sailing away through the air with their horses, until most of them disappeared into the blue of the sky, or beyond the far mountains. A small sergeant called out for mercy; so the blower blew more softly and allowed him to float gently to the ground. 'Go and tell the king,' he said, 'that if he sends any more troops they will all be blown over the hills and far away.'

Then the six took their treasure home and shared it equally between them, and they lived happily for the rest of their lives.

The Cockerel-stone

In the city of Grottanegra there once lived a man called Aniello. His wordly possessions consisted of a single cockerel, which he had reared from a chick; but the time came when he was so poor that he had to sell it in order to buy food.

In the market he met two sorcerers who offered him a good price for the cockerel, and it was agreed that Aniello should take it to their house, where he would be paid. As they walked along, the sorcerers whispered together. 'How fortunate that this simpleton does not know why we are buying his cockerel!' said one. 'We can make all our wishes come true with the magic stone from its head!'

But Aniello had overheard what they were saying. He made off at once with his precious cockerel, and as soon as he reached home he killed it. He took the stone from its head, and set it in a brass ring. Now he could test its magical powers. 'I wish I were a young lad of eighteen years old!' he said.

Scarcely had the words left his lips than he felt new strength flow through his tired old limbs, and found that he was a handsome young fellow of eighteen. Next he wished for a palace, and for a princess to be his bride. In the twinkling of an eye a palace of unbelievable beauty stood before him. Magnificent halls glittered with silver and with gold, and there were any number of servants. In short, everything was so magnificent that the princess's father had not the slightest hesitation in permitting Aniello to marry his lovely daughter.

Some years later, when the two sorcerers discovered how lucky Aniello had been, they planned to rob him of his magic stone. With great skill they made a beautiful doll which could both sing and dance, disguised themselves as merchants, and paid a visit to Pentella, Aniello's little daughter.

Pentella was entranced by the beautiful doll, and longed to possess it. The false merchants whispered to her, 'You may keep the doll if you will let us see your father's ring.' Pentella wanted the doll so much that she promised to bring them the ring on the following morning. She stroked and curled her father's beard, and at last persuaded him to let her keep the ring for just one day.

Next morning the sorcerers returned, and no sooner had the ring touched their hands than they disappeared in a cloud of smoke. As soon as they reached a nearby forest they ordered the ring to undo all Aniello's wishes.

Aniello was talking to the king when the sorcerers made their wish. Suddenly his hair was white and sparse, and his features wrinkled. In a flash all his fine clothes were replaced by the rags and tatters he had worn before his wishes came true.

The king ordered the ragged old man to be taken from his presence, and in despair Aniello hurried to his daughter to ask for his ring, so that he could make good this stroke of ill-fortune. When he learned of the trick that had been played on the innocent child by the two false merchants, he made up his mind to search the whole world until he found them and his precious ring. He put on his old cloak and a pair of wooden clogs, took up his bundle and set off.

At last his wanderings brought him to the kingdom of Deep-Hole, which was inhabited by mice. The mice suspected him of being a spy for the cats, so he was taken prisoner and led before King Gnaw-well. On being questioned, Aniello first gave the king a piece of bacon-rind as a token of goodwill, and then related his whole sad story.

King Gnaw-well felt sorry for Aniello in his misfortune, and called on his wisest counsellors to advise how Aniello might be helped to find the missing sorcerers. Amongst the counsellors were two mice, called Bite-well and Leap-well, who had recently returned from six years spent in an inn by a main highway. They had seen a great deal there, and, only a short while before, they had overheard two men from Castell Rampino talking of how they had cheated an old man of his magic stone. One of them, called Januarius, had said, 'I will never take the ring from my finger. That would be courting disaster – like the old fool who lost it by giving it to his little daughter for a day!'

When Aniello heard these words, he asked the two mice if they would be willing to help him regain possession of the ring, promising to reward them with as much cheese and bacon as they wanted. The mice agreed immediately when they heard of this rich reward, and promised to follow him over land and sea if necessary.

After a long journey they came to Castell Rampino. The two mice left Aniello hiding in a copse while they went to spy out the land. They had to resort to cunning, however, as Januarius never removed the ring from his finger.

They waited until it was night, and as soon as Januarius had gone to bed Bite-well slipped between the sheets and began to gnaw the sorcerer's ring-finger. The sorcerer was soon in pain, and took off the ring, laying it on his bedside table. As soon as Leap-well saw this, he leapt on the ring, seized it between his teeth, and scampered away with Bite-well as fast as his tiny legs could carry him.

Aniello could hardly believe his good fortune. With Leap-well and Bite-well he returned to the kingdom of Deep-hole, where he gave King Gnaw-well and his counsellors a magnificent banquet of cheese and bacon. He thanked them from the bottom of his heart for all their help, and prayed that no cat would ever harm them.

Wasting no time on his return journey to Grottanegra, Aniello hurried – once again in the form of a strong and handsome youth – to pay his respects to the king and the princess, who were overjoyed to see him. He lived for many years in great happiness with his beautiful wife, but never again did he remove the ring from his finger.

Five in a Pod

Five peas lay together in a pod. They were green and the pod was green, and so they thought that the whole world was green, and that was quite right. The pod grew, and the peas grew. The sun outside warmed the pod, and the rain made it clear and translucent. As the peas grew bigger they began to wonder why they were lying in a row, and what would happen to them in the end.

'Are we to lie here for ever?' they said. 'We shall become quite hard if we stay here much longer. There must be something more exciting in store for us.'

Weeks passed by. The peas turned yellow, and the pod turned yellow. 'The whole world has turned yellow!' they declared, and they were quite right.

Suddenly they felt a jerk. The pod was torn from the plant, and stuffed into a coat-pocket, together with a number of other pods. 'Now we shall soon be opened,' they whispered expectantly.

'I am curious to see which of us will do best in the world,' said the smallest pea. 'Not long to wait now!'

Pop! The pod burst, and all five peas rolled out into the bright sunshine. They lay in a little boy's hand, and the little boy thought they looked just right for his pop-gun. He loaded the first pea and shot it into the air.

'Here I am on my way to seek my fortune,' cried the pea.

'I'm going to fly to the sun,' shouted the second pea, as he shot up into the sky.

'We are going to sleep,' said the third and fourth, 'just

as soon as we fall to the ground.' And they fell from the boy's hand and rolled away. But the little boy picked them up and loaded them both together. 'We are going the furthest after all!' they cried.

'Who knows what will happen to me!' said the fifth, as he sailed through the air.

He landed on the rotting wooden sill of a little attic window, where he lodged in a crack filled with moss and soft brown earth. He lay hidden there for a long time, but not forgotten by God.

In the attic room lived a poor woman, who went out each day to earn her living. She cleaned out fire-places, swept rooms, scrubbed floors, and chopped wood; but even though she worked so hard, she was always poor. While she was out working, her little daughter stayed at home in the attic. She had been lying ill for a whole year, hovering between life and death. 'Perhaps she wants to join her sister with God,' said the poor woman. 'But I *do* want to keep her with me, if God will grant it.'

Early one morning the following spring the poor mother was about to leave for work. The sun was shining warmly through the little attic window, and the sick child was gazing at the sunbeams. Suddenly she noticed something, and cried, 'What is that green thing peeping up at the corner of the window-pane? It's waving in the wind!'

Her mother opened the window and looked out. 'Well!' she exclaimed, 'It is a little pea which has sprouted. How in the world can it have found its way up here? Now you have a little garden to look after.' And she moved her daughter's bed nearer to the window, so that she could look out at the little pea-plant more easily.

When the poor woman came home from work that

evening, her daughter said, 'Mother, I think I am going to get well. The sun has been shining in on me all day, the little pea feels happy and is growing bigger, and I feel much better. I shall soon be getting up and going out into the fresh air.'

'Yes, of course, dear,' said the poor mother, grateful to the little pea for giving her daughter such happy thoughts. She stuck a little cane into the wooden window-sill and tied the pea-plant to it, to prevent it from being broken by the wind. Then she stretched a length of thread from the window-sill to the roof, so that the tendrils could climb up it. Every day they could see the little pea-plant grow bigger.

'Oh, look!' cried the little girl one day. 'It has flowers!'

Indeed it had, and the mother began to hope that her sick child might recover. Certainly she looked a great deal better, particularly when she sat up in bed and watched the little plant, her eyes gleaming with excitement.

The following week the little girl managed to leave her bed for the first time, and she sat happily for a whole hour in the warm sunshine at the open window, tending her tiny garden of a single pea-plant. The delicate pink and white blossom glowed in the sunlight and the little girl tenderly kissed the little green leaves.

The mother smiled happily at the plant, as though it were an angel from heaven. 'God must have made it grow here to fill us both with joy and hope,' she thought.

What happened to the other four peas? Well, the first one landed in the gutter. In a trice it was gobbled up by a pigeon, and lay inside its stomach like Jonah inside the whale. The two lazy peas, who had wanted only to sleep,

fared no better, for they too were swallowed by pigeons. But all three were at least of some use in this way.

The pea who had wanted to fly right to the sun landed in a drain and lay soaking in the dirty water. Days passed by, and weeks and months, and it swelled and swelled until it had almost reached bursting point. 'No pea could possibly grow bigger than me!' it exclaimed with pride. 'I must be the best of the five!' And the drain agreed.

But up at the attic window the little girl stood with sparkling eyes, and with the bloom of health on her cheeks. She cupped her hands tenderly round the delicate pea-blossom and gave thanks to God.

The Little Match-girl

It was snowing and the wind blew cold as darkness fell over the city. It was New Year's Eve. In the gathering gloom a little girl with bare feet padded through the streets. She had been wearing her mother's slippers when she left home, but they were far too big, and she had lost them while hurrying across a busy road. One of them was nowhere to be found, and a little boy had run off with the other. So now her bare feet were mottled blue and red with the bitter cold.

In her old apron the little girl carried bundles of matches which her father had sent her out to sell, but all day long nobody had bought a single match from her. Cold and hungry, she made her weary way through the city. Brilliant lights streamed from the windows of big houses, where blazing fires crackled merrily in the hearth, and the smell of roast goose hung on the air, for it was New Year's Eve.

The little girl crouched down in a corner between two houses. She drew her knees up to her chest, but this seemed to make her even colder. She was afraid to go home, for she had sold nothing the whole day! Not a penny had she earned, and her father would surely be angry with her. But it was just as cold at home, for the wind whistled through the cracks in the walls and floorboards.

How wonderful it would be to light a match! All she had to do was to take one out of its bundle, strike it on the wall, and warm her fingers at the flame. She drew out a match and struck it. How it sparkled and gleamed! How the flames leapt and the shadows danced! It seemed to the little girl as if she were sitting by an enormous iron stove with brass ornaments on it. She stretched out her frozen feet to warm them – and the flame went out. Gone was the wonderful stove, and there she sat in the snow with the burnt-out match smoking between her fingers.

She struck another. The match flared up, making a new circle of brightness. The light fell on the stone wall, which immediately became as transparent as gauze. She found herself looking into a cosy room, where a table stood spread with a white linen tablecloth and set with silver, while in the middle steamed an enormous roast goose. The goose leapt out of the dish and began to waddle towards her – and the match went out. She saw nothing but the cold, grey wall before her.

Once again she struck a match, and found herself sitting at the foot of a magnificent Christmas tree. Thousands of tiny candles twinkled on the tips of the green branches, and brilliant paper streamers and tinsel hung down to the floor. The little girl stretched both her hands towards it – and the match went out. The candles seemed to climb higher and higher, until she saw that they were the cold, bright stars above her. One of them fell across the wintry sky, drawing a long fiery tail behind it. Someone must be dying, she thought, for her old grandmother, who had always been so kind to her, had said, 'Whenever you see a falling star, you will know that a soul is on its way to God!'

She struck another match. It threw a warm circle of light all round her, and within the bright circle stood her grandmother, smiling gently down at her.

'Oh, Grandmother,' cried the poor girl, 'take me with

you, please! I know I shall never see you again once the match burns out. You will vanish just as the warm stove, the roast goose, and the beautiful Christmas tree did!' Quickly she struck the remaining matches, one after the other, for she did not want her grandmother to disappear.

Never had her grandmother looked so kind. She gathered the little girl into her arms and swept her up to heaven. How bright everything was! Here she felt neither cold, nor hunger, nor fear – for they were with God.

Early next day the people found the little match-girl huddled against the wall, the spent matches scattered about her. She was dead – but there was a smile of happiness on her lips.

'Poor soul, she was trying to warm herself,' the people said; but no one guessed what beautiful things the little match-girl had seen by the light of her matches, nor how happy she was with her grandmother that glorious New Year's morning.

The Sunshade

Agatha was the daughter of a rich goldsmith, and lived in a grand house which had a great many rooms and sweeping staircases, and a fine, large garden. Her father gave her as many gold rings and bracelets as she wanted, and her wardrobe was full to overflowing with beautiful dresses of silk and bright satin. But she took no joy in all these things, for she was very ugly. All day she would wander about the house or pick flowers in the garden, not daring to go out into the streets until the dusk was falling.

One day the housekeeper who looked after the gold-smith's house fell ill and Agatha had to go to the market in broad daylight in order to buy meat and vegetables. She pulled her bonnet frills over her forehead, so that no one should see her ugly face, but the women in the market-place all recognized her and whispered to each other, 'Look, there goes the goldsmith's daughter. It's true – she really is as ugly as they say!'

Agatha passed quickly between the stalls. She hated to hear people making fun of her, and wished she were safe at home.

Suddenly she heard an old woman calling after her, 'Where are you going in such a hurry, Agatha? Come and see my wares.'

The voice sounded kind enough, so Agatha paused and looked round.

'That's better,' said the old woman. 'Come here, my child. I have something to show you.'

She rummaged in an old hamper, pulled out a sun-shade and opened it up. It was of delicate, pale-blue silk embroidered with tiny white pearls. 'Do you like it?' she asked.

'Oh yes,' replied Agatha. 'But I spend most of my time indoors, so I have no use for a sunshade.'

The old woman smiled. 'One moment,' she said. 'Hold the sunshade over your head and take a look at yourself!' A mirror gleamed in the old woman's wrinkled hand, and Agatha saw reflected in it the face of a beautiful stranger.

'There you are!' said the old woman. 'As long as you hold the sunshade over your head nothing but the beauty of your kind heart will be seen, and no one will dream of laughing at you.'

'If it were only mine,' the girl sighed, stroking the blue silk.

'It *is* yours, my child,' said the old woman. 'I have given it to you. Go now, and be happy.'

Agatha could see that the old woman was poor, and could ill afford to give presents, so she took a gold bracelet from her arm and handed it to her saying, 'May I give you something too, to bring you happiness?'

So she went on her way. As she passed shyly through the market-place she felt the admiring glances of the passers-by, and she smiled happily under the blue dome of the sunshade.

As she entered the house she closed the sunshade, and once again she saw her ugly features looking back at her from the hall mirror. I will not tell Father anything about it, she thought. How sad he would be to see me beautiful one moment and ugly the next. So she hid the old woman's gift in a cupboard, and carried on with her work as though nothing had happened.

Before dusk fell Agatha put on a pretty silk dress and left the house. She did not care if people thought it strange for her to be carrying a sunshade when the sun had already set: she wanted to be beautiful! But everyone was so charmed by her loveliness that the sunshade went unnoticed. Long after she had passed by, people were still talking about the beautiful stranger.

There was a big park in the city, where a band played every evening beneath bright coloured lights. Agatha had always longed to join in the dancing there, but she had never dared. Now she felt no fear, and danced merrily beneath the fragrant acacia blossoms, gaily whirling the blue sunshade over her head.

All the young men of the city who had previously avoided Agatha now crowded round to talk with her, eager to know whether she were on a short visit to the city, or whether she meant to stay. She wandered happily past the fountains and through the rose-gardens with her admirers, talking and joking with sparkling eyes, until she heard a sudden burst of coarse, cruel laughter.

She stopped in dismay. Had the sunshade lost its magic power? Was she ugly again, and were the people laughing at her? Surely not – all her companions were as attentive as ever. A moment later she saw that a crowd had gathered round a poor hunchback. People were tugging at his clothes and yelling, 'Go away! You're spoiling our fun, you ugly creature!'

'We must help him,' said Agatha. 'What harm has he done?' She forced a way between the dancers and said,

'Leave the poor fellow alone! Have you no thought for other people's feelings?'

'But just look how ugly he is,' shrieked a girl. 'The horrid dwarf!'

Agatha stood silent for a moment, and then she handed the old hunchback her magic sunshade. His features at once became youthful and bright, his back straightened, and he stood noble and tall. His persecutors stepped back in amazement. Agatha hung her head, thinking that all their scorn would now descend on her; but no one seemed to notice her, so astonished were they at the miraculous transformation of the ugly hunchback.

The man still held the sunshade over his head, unable to understand what had happened to him. Agatha held out her hand to take it back, but felt all at once that she no longer wanted it. Without a word she turned and walked away through the park. One by one the bright lights went out, but there was a full moon to light the paths, and the surface of the pond glittered between the silent banks. Agatha bent down to cool her brow with the cold water. But – was this her true reflection? A beautiful face, radiant with goodness, looked up at her from the deep mirror of the pond. It was even more beautiful than it had been under the sunshade. The stars twinkled in the water, and the breeze carried them on the waves, like thousands of little diamonds, to where Agatha knelt on the bank.

The Magic Horse

Many years ago there reigned a king of Persia called Sabur, who was the greatest and most powerful of all the rulers of his time. Every year he celebrated two festivals – Niraj, the feast of the New Year, and Mirjan, the feast of the autumn equinox. At these times he threw open his palaces to all his subjects, and set his prisoners free.

Now it came about that on one of these festivals an Indian sorcerer came to him with a priceless gift, a horse of blackest ebony, with trappings of gold set with precious stones. The king was most impressed with the skilled and delicate craftsmanship, but he could not help asking what was the use of such a creature.

'My lord,' replied the sorcerer, 'this horse can travel with its rider as far in one day as any normal horse can travel in a year, for it flies through the air.'

'By Allah,' said the king, 'if it is the truth you speak, I promise to grant you any request you wish to make.'

The sorcerer immediately swung into the saddle, and the horse rose several feet into the air. The king was delighted, and said, 'I see that you have spoken the truth. Now I must fulfil my part of the bargain. Name your reward.'

Now the sorcerer had heard that the king had a beautiful daughter. 'My lord and master,' he said, 'I should like your daughter as my bride.'

'So be it,' replied the king.

Meantime the princess had been standing behind a curtain and had heard everything. She had also seen that her

husband-to-be was very old, with a face that was furrowed with a million wrinkles, while she was young and graceful, dainty and gentle as a gazelle, lovelier than the new moon.

The princess ran to her room and threw herself down, weeping bitterly. And that is how her brother, Prince Akmar, found her on his return from hunting. 'What is the matter?' he asked.

'Alas, dear brother,' she replied. 'Our father intends to give me in marriage to an ugly old sorcerer who has deceived him with a magic gift. But I will not be his bride. Can you not help me, brother?'

Her brother promised to do his best and hurried to his father, the king. 'What is this I hear about a sorcerer?' he said. 'And what is the present he has given you?'

'When you have seen the horse,' replied the king, 'you too will be amazed.' And he ordered his servants to bring the horse. The prince leapt nimbly into the saddle, and

dug his spurs into the horse's flanks; but the horse did not budge from the spot.

The king called the sorcerer, saying, 'Show my son how the horse works; then he will understand that I cannot refuse to grant your wish.'

The sorcerer quickly realized that Prince Akmar was no friend of his, and showed him a lever on the horse's right side. As soon as the lever was pulled, he said, the horse would take to the air. So the prince pulled it, and the horse took to the air and flew away, and soon it was only the tiniest spot in the distance.

The king was worried for his son's safety. 'How can he bring the horse back to earth?' he asked.

'My lord,' exclaimed the sorcerer angrily, 'is it my fault if you never see him again till the end of the world? He did not ask me how to bring it back to earth. I simply showed him what he *did* ask me.'

The king was greatly angered and had the sorcerer thrown into prison. He tore the crown from his head, beat his breast, and wept. What a sad end to all the gay festivities! The palace gates were locked and bolted, and the whole city sank into the deepest mourning for the lost prince.

Meanwhile the prince had been carried up to the sun on the ebony horse, and was almost dead from the fierce heat. Before I faint away, he thought, I must look quickly to see if there is not a lever to make the horse descend. He reached with his hand down the horse's left flank, and there indeed was a second lever. He pulled it, and the horse began to descend. Soon the earth came into view, and the prince spied a great palace behind some trees. He flew the horse towards it and landed quietly on a balcony. By this time night was falling. He found a staircase which led downwards to a vestibule with walls of white marble. He looked about him and saw a light gleaming where a door had been left ajar. Softly he pushed the door open and took a few paces into the room. To his amazement the whole floor was covered with sleeping men, each with an unsheathed sabre at his side. From this he concluded that he was in the antechamber of a princess's boudoir, and that the sleeping men must be her bodyguard.

On tiptoe Prince Akmar approached a delicate silk curtain which hung over a doorway at the far side of the room. He lifted the curtain, and stepped into a cool, airy chamber. A number of low beds stood ranged round the walls, while in the middle of the room, set on a dais of white ivory, was a bed with hangings of rich silk. Here lay the princess, while her maids slept on the lower beds. Prince Akmar went quietly up to the princess, and pulled gently at her sleeve.

The princess opened her eyes. At first she was so surprised at the sight of a stranger in her boudoir that she was unable to utter a word. The prince took advantage of her silence to bow his forehead until it touched the floor, saying, 'Most gracious princess, here at your feet lies the son of the King of Persia, brought here by a most extraordinary adventure, and now in deadly peril of his life unless you will be kind and generous enough to give him your help and protection.'

'Have no fear, dear prince,' replied the princess. 'Here in the kingdom of Bengal we respect the laws of hospitality just as you do in Persia.' With these words she wakened her maids, and ordered them to prepare food and wine for the prince, and to make a bed ready for him.

Prince Akmar slept long and soundly, and had just finished dressing himself next morning when the princess sent one of her maids to warn him that she was about to visit him. After mutual greetings he gave the princess a detailed account of his strange adventure. When he had finished, she said, 'Although I see you safe and sound before me, I feared for your safety all the time you were talking, until you told me how your horse landed so easily on the palace balcony.'

The prince was delighted that she was so sympathetic towards him, and asked her name. 'Shems al Nahar,' she replied, which means Midday Sun. They talked together happily for many hours, and it was no wonder that Prince Akmar soon became so enchanted by the beauty and grace of his hostess that he fell head over heels in love with her.

Before nightfall he had confessed his love to her, and had asked her to be his bride. Nothing could have pleased her better, and as there was no reason to doubt that their parents would be delighted they saw no obstacle to their happiness.

The prince said he would like to take his bride to the Persian court the very next day, for he wanted to set his parents' mind at rest as to what had happened to him, and to win their approval for his wedding with the Princess of Bengal. But although he assured her that the ebony horse travelled swiftly enough to take them to Persia and back in a single day, the princess insisted that he should first visit *her* father, to ask for her hand in marriage, as well as his permission to go to the Persian court.

They mounted the ebony horse together, and in next to no time they were in the king's palace. He gave them a great welcome, and raised no objection either to their wedding or to their immediate journey to Persia.

The sun had barely risen above the distant horizon on the following morning when the prince mounted the magic horse with his beloved who clung to him as the horse took to the air. Soon they were high in the blue vault of the sky, travelling faster than the wind.

Three hours later they were over the capital of Persia. Prince Akmar brought the ebony horse gently to the ground in a garden outside the city. He helped the princess down and led her by the hand into a little summerhouse, saying, 'Wait here for a short while. I will go and tell my parents of our arrival. They will send the Vizir and the whole army in full regalia to welcome you to Persia.' And off he went alone.

He found his mother, father, and sister in robes of

mourning for they were sure he had been killed. They ran to meet him with open arms, and asked amid tears of joy what had happened to him. Great was the rejoicing! The news of his return soon spread through the whole city, and the streets rang with shouts of jubilation. Trumpets sounded and cymbals clashed, and the mourning robes were changed for garments of rejoicing. The whole city was hung with banners and streamers, and thousands of people thronged the palace gates. The king ordered a week's festivities with banquets for all the people, and set all his prisoners free. Soon a joyful procession was on its way to the garden where Akmar had left the Bengali princess.

Meantime the wicked sorcerer, who had been set free with the other prisoners, swore a terrible revenge on Prince Akmar. He hurried on ahead of the procession and found the princess in the summerhouse, with the ebony horse tethered not far away.

The young prince crossed me because of his sister, he thought bitterly. Now I will repay him in his own coin and take away his bride on the ebony horse.

He knocked lightly on the summerhouse door.

'Who's there?' asked the princess.

'Your slave and faithful servant,' the sorcerer replied. 'Your prince has sent me to bring you to him. I am to take you to the palace on the magic horse, for Her Majesty the queen is eager to welcome you.'

The princess had not the slightest suspicion of his wickedness, and opened the door without a moment's hesitation. But when she saw the ugly and evil-looking old man she hesitated, and said, 'Has the queen no better servant than you to conduct me to her?'

'My queen has hundreds of fine-looking servants,' replied the sorcerer. 'But I am her oldest and most faithful servant, and so she sent me.'

The princess believed him, and mounted the ebony horse. The sorcerer mounted behind her and pulled the lever. The horse immediately rose into the air, circled round, and headed towards China.

At that very moment the procession from the palace arrived in the garden – the prince and princess with the king and the queen, followed by hundreds of troops arrayed in glorious colours, playing trumpets and beating cymbals and drums to welcome the Bengali princess to Persia. The prince stepped into the summerhouse to bring out his beloved. But the room was empty. In despair he flung his turban on the ground and began to beat his breast, and for a long time he would not be comforted. Then he thought to ask the gardener who else had been in the garden that morning. 'Only the Indian sorcerer,' replied the gardener.

Prince Akmar knew at once that the sorcerer had stolen his princess. But what could he do? He thought for some time, and then he turned to his father the king, saying, 'Go back to the palace. I do not yet know what I shall do, but I will not move from this spot till I have found a solution.' So the king and the whole procession turned and wended their way slowly and sadly back to the city. Rejoicing turned once more to mourning.

Meantime the sorcerer had reached China with the Bengali princess, and had landed beside a stream in a luxuriant green valley. 'Where is your master?' asked the princess. 'And where are his parents and sister?'

'Allah curse them all!' hissed the sorcerer. 'I am your

master now. This is *my* horse – I made it. You shall never see your prince again. But do not fear. I have endless riches, and I will give you all the fine clothes you desire and fulfill your every wish.' He spoke thus, thinking to win her for his bride, but she would have none of him, and pushed him away with loud cries and weeping.

Now the Emperor of China was hunting in the valley at that time. He saw the poor girl weeping by the side of the stream, and wondered at her beauty. He kicked the sorcerer, who had fallen asleep, and asked, 'Who is this woman?'

'She is my wife, Your Majesty,' replied the sorcerer.

At these words the princess leapt to her feet and kissed the emperor's stirrup. 'He is lying, my lord. He is a wicked sorcerer who has deceived me and abducted me.'

'Seize the old man,' ordered the Emperor of China, 'and throw him into my deepest dungeon.' And the emperor's servants carried out their lord's command.

The emperor turned back towards the city with the Bengali princess, and on the way he asked her to tell him about the ebony horse. 'Indeed, my lord,' she cried, 'it is a most wonderful horse, for it can travel great distances faster than the wind.' When the emperor heard that, he ordered his servant to put the horse safely in the imperial treasury.

The emperor was pleased and happy, and as soon as he reached his palace he had the princess shown to a magnificent chamber. That very evening he visited her, and told her that he wanted to marry her. The princess still thought of Prince Akmar, however, and would not listen to him. To escape his demands she pretended that she was mad. She beat her face with her hands, stamped her feet,

and tore her clothes to the accompaniment of shrill cries. The emperor was sadly perplexed and left her apartment after giving instruction that she was to be carefully looked after by all his maid-servants, doctors, and astrologers.

Meanwhile Prince Akmar journeyed disconsolately from country to country, and in time the all-seeing and all-hearing Allah guided his footsteps to the capital city of China. In the bazaar there he heard the market-people talking of a beautiful girl in the palace, who was out of her wits. He asked them how she had come to the palace, and when he heard their story he had little doubt that the girl was indeed his beloved.

He was overjoyed but cautious, so he disguised himself as an astrologer. He fashioned for himself flowing robes inscribed with magic symbols, and an immense turban for his head. He blackened his eyebrows and combed his beard, and altogether gave himself a most imposing appearance. He took a roll of fine parchment and a little box of sand, and presented himself at the palace. 'Tell the emperor that I am a wise astrologer, come all the way from Persia,' he said to the doorkeeper. 'I have heard of his slave's madness, and I am certain that I can cure it.' Quickly the doorkeeper let him in, and took him straight to the emperor.

Prince Akmar conducted himself like a real astrologer, muttering words which no one could understand, as he bowed deeply before the emperor and touched the ground with his forehead.

'Oh, wise one,' said the emperor, 'I have had the girl here for more than a year. She is for ever stamping her feet and beating the air with her arms, and nothing can make her stop. If you can cure her I will give you whatever you want.'

'Take me to her,' said the prince. 'First I must see her, in order to discover what manner of evil spirits have taken possession of her.'

The emperor ordered his servants to take the disguised prince into the princess's apartment, so that he might examine her. As he stood outside her door he heard the sound of weeping. He was sore at heart as he stepped quickly inside, and said, 'May Allah be merciful to you, Shems al Nahar! With his help you will soon be rescued. I am Akmar!'

As soon as she heard his voice the princess raised her eyes. With amazement and delight she recognized him through his disguise, and leapt to her feet. She threw herself into his arms and kissed him. 'But how in the world did you find me here?' she asked. 'There is no time to talk now,' he replied, 'for I still do not know how I am to take you away from here. But I shall soon find a way!' Reluctantly he turned and left her, and went back to the emperor. 'Your Majesty,' he declared, 'I will show you a miracle!'

The emperor rose and returned with Akmar to the princess's apartment. As soon as they entered she began to scream, and to brandish her arms and stamp her feet. Akmar went up to her and made magic passes with his hands over her face, and muttered incantations, whispering softly, 'Go quietly now to the emperor, kiss his hand, and show yourself compliant with his wishes.' After Akmar had made a few more magic signs with his hands the princess fell to the ground as if unconscious, and lay there motionless for several minutes. Suddenly she stirred as if she had just awakened out of a long sleep. Quietly she stood up, and went dutifully to the emperor, saying, 'Welcome, my lord and master. How gracious of you to visit your humble slave today!'

The emperor was beside himself with joy when he heard these words. He turned to the prince, and said, 'Ask for whatever you want. I grant it to you in advance.'

'No, Your Majesty,' replied the prince. 'It is not yet time for my reward, for I fear the malady will break out afresh unless we act quickly. You must have her carefully bathed by ten slave-girls, but her feet must not be allowed to touch the ground. Then she must be arrayed in the costliest apparel, so that her heart will forget all its misery. And finally you must have her taken back to the place where you found her, for that is where the evil spirit entered into her.'

The emperor lost no time in carrying out the prince's

advice. The whole court and the imperial guard followed the emperor, the prince, and the Bengali princess to the banks of the stream where she had first landed on her arrival from Persia. The prince muttered incantations, made mysterious signs with his hands, burnt incense, and watched the smoke formations as they rose into the sky.

After a while he approached the emperor, and said, 'Your Majesty, it is clear to me that the evil spirit which has taken possession of this woman belongs properly to a certain animal carved out of black ebony. Unless this animal can be found. so that I can send the evil spirit back into it, I fear the lady cannot be properly or permanently cured of her madness.'

'You must indeed be the wisest of men,' said the emperor, 'the most brilliant astrologer I have ever met. For with my own eyes I saw a black ebony horse standing on the banks of this very stream where I first found the girl. Perhaps that is the animal which you have in mind?'

The emperor at once gave orders for the horse to be brought to him. The prince examined it carefully, in order to be quite certain that it had suffered no damage. Then he gave instructions for a ring of incense cones to be lit all round the horse. When all was wreathed in thick smoke Akmar lifted the princess on to the horse, leapt into the saddle before her, and pulled the lever. As the horse soared high into the air above the heads of the court, the emperor cried, 'Stop them! Stop them at once!' But what could anyone do?

Prince Akmar called down to him, 'Next time you want to marry a princess who has asked for your protection, do not forget to ask first if she wants to marry *you*!'

Swift as the wind they flew through the air, and in next

to no time they landed on the steps before the palace of the Persian king. Like lightning the news of their happy arrival spread through the city, and all the people gave thanks to Allah, the All-powerful. All the citizens, the viziers, and the royal troops turned out to welcome them and wish them joy. Messengers were sent to fetch the bride's father all the way from Bengal, and he brought with him many costly and beautiful presents for the happy couple.

The whole city was decked out with streamers and coloured lanterns. The wedding lasted for seven days and seven nights, and much money was distributed to the poor. The magic horse was put safely in the royal treasury. But no one was quite so happy as the prince and his Bengali princess.

Little Step-mother

There was once a king whose beloved wife died, and he mourned her for many a long year. But the time came when he realized that his two daughters were growing up wild and spoilt through lack of a mother's care, and so he married again. His new wife brought him two daughters of her own. A great many of the nobles and court servants were not at all pleased at the king's marriage, for they had been very fond of his first wife. His two daughters were particularly loud in their protests, and behaved abominably towards their step-mother, declaring that she treated them far more harshly than her own two daughters.

Now the wise Mistress Goodly, a fair and gentle judge, heard these complaints while she was on her way through the king's territory with her daughter, Mother Holle. She decided to investigate for herself, and sent Mother Holle on alone. She disguised herself as a lady-in-waiting and entered into the queen's service. She stayed for some time, keenly watching all that went on around her, and she found the new queen was doing her very best to treat all four daughters equally. She was a kind and dutiful young wife, loving and sympathetic and completely devoted to the king, her daughters, and her step-daughters.

Mistress Goodly was satisfied – she was always glad to find people better than their reputations – and went on her way.

The following year Mother Holle passed that way by herself. She soon discovered that the queen's step-daughters were still complaining, and that many of the people of that country were only too ready to believe that the queen was treating them badly. Mother Holle was angry that such a state of affairs should be allowed to continue. She saw the step-daughters dressed in rags (in order to win sympathy), and the queen's own two daughters in their pretty, delicate clothes, and she determined to put an end to the strife once and for all.

She sent for the queen and the four girls, and turned them all into one flower – for she was particularly fond of creating new flowers for her garden. The queen became the lowest petal, with the two brightly dressed daughters next to her and the more plainly dressed step-daughters at the top. Mother Holle was sure that this transformation would serve as a warning to all quarrelsome people. She planted the little flower firmly in the soft earth, called it Little Step-mother, and continued on her way to her gardens by the sea.

The king grew sad and lonely, for he did not know what had become of his wife and daughters. Then one day he heard a rumour that his five loved ones had been turned into a new flower called a pansy or Little Step-mother, and it was certain that no one had ever set eyes on such a flower before the disappearance of his wife and four daughters. His hopes were high as he dug up the little flower and planted it in his garden. He tried to ask it what had become of his wife and children, but the little flower answered not a word.

Summer passed and turned to autumn. The long dark nights of winter gave way to spring. In May Mistress Goodly came back on her rounds, and paid her annual visit to the kingdom. The king soon heard of her arrival, and took his complaint to her. That is how the kindly judge heard of the poor king's grief. It did not take her long to guess who was responsible for the mischief.

For the time being she said nothing, but disguised herself once again and prolonged her stay in that country, sending her servants through the land to discover what the people really thought about the queen and her children. She heard what everyone had to say, and then one night she stood by the pansy, Little Step-mother, and called the five bewitched people by their names. One by one they stepped out of the flower, in their own human forms – Mistress Goodly had the power to deal with Mother Holle's mischief.

'Do you like your new dwelling-place?' she asked. The two step-daughters said nothing; and the two daughters wept without attempting to answer her. The queen, however, replied gently, 'I was so careful to treat them all equally. Can nothing be done to comfort the king in his loneliness?'

'Is that all you have to say?' asked Mistress Goodly.

'No', replied the poor queen. 'Let the children go back. They are wasting their young lives here.'

'Which of them do you want me to send back to the court?' asked Mistress Goodly impatiently.

'All four of them,' implored the queen. 'They will all bring joy and comfort to the king.'

Mistress Goodly was glad that the queen bore no grudge against her step-daughters, and she instructed one of the servants to take the queen and her four daughters to the king. At the same time, however, she gave her blessing to the little flower which Mother Holle had created, and instructed it how to grow and bear seeds.

That is how the pansy, Little Step-mother, came into this world. It reminds Mother Holle of her over-hasty judgment, and it reminds us of the unjustified complaints of selfish and jealous people. For many years after, the King ruled happily over his people. Peace and contentment reigned throughout the court and the whole land and the king and queen loved one another for the rest of their lives.

The Five Brothers Li

By the yellow waters of the great river Yangtze Kiang lived a good woman who had five sons, the five brothers Li. They were called Li the First, Li the Second, Li the Third, Li the Fourth, and Li the Fifth. These brother looked so much alike that their mother could hardly tell them apart, yet each had a special gift that was not shared by the others. Li the First could drink the whole sea at a gulp and spout it forth again in a gushing torrent. Li the Second could not be burnt by fire. Li the Third could make his legs grow as

long as he wanted. Li the Fourth had a body as hard as steel. And the youngest of the brothers, Li the Fifth, understood the languages of all the animals, birds, and fishes as well as he understood his own Chinese mother-tongue.

The brothers were the best of friends. Li the First caught fishes, Li the Second stoked the fire with his hands, Li the Third and Li the Fourth worked in the fields, while Li the Fifth looked after the sheep and the geese.

One day a high-ranking mandarin came to hunt by the waters of the Yangtze Kiang. A little shepherd-boy sat at the edge of a wood, tending a flock of sheep and four geese: this was Li the Fifth. Beside him lay a beautiful spotted mountain goat, sunning itself peacefully and without a shadow of fear. Quick as lightning the wicked man-

darin drew his bow and took careful aim at the little goat
as it lay blinking its eyes lazily in the sun. Suddenly Li saw
the mandarin and leapt to his feet, shouting to the goat to
run, and it disappeared into the wood with one bound.
Next moment a stag came through the trees. and Li yelled
to it in deer language, 'Quick! Run away and save yourself!' And the great stag vanished like a flash.

Li was glad that he had been able to help his woodland
friends, but the mandarin, once he had got over his astonishment, was furious. Livid with rage, he ordered his servants to seize Li. He was dragged to the city, where he was
flung into a cage with a hungry tiger. The mandarin had
expected the tiger to tear the miserable shepherd-boy limb
from limb, but Li spoke to the beast in tiger language and
it drew in its claws immediately. It allowed Li to pat it and

to scratch it behind its ears and soon it was purring loudly, just like a big cat.

The mandarin's fury knew no bounds, and he ordered his men to take Li away and chop off his head.

While Li the Fifth sat in prison awaiting his execution, Li the Fourth crept quietly in and changed places with him. You will remember that Li the Fourth's body was as hard as steel. The two brothers looked so much alike, that not one of the mandarin's men noticed the change which had taken place.

Next morning Li the Fourth was led out to be executed. The executioner raised his sword high above his head and brought it down with terrific force on Li's neck. The sword was razor-sharp and of the highest quality, but it split into a thousand fragments on Li's neck, which was of course as hard as steel.

The fearsome mandarin grew angrier than ever, and ordered his men to hurl Li over a high cliff. During the night, however, Li the Third – the Li who could make his legs as long as he wanted – changed places with Li the Fourth, and once again no one noticed the difference.

At first light on the following morning Li was taken up to the top of a high cliff. The mandarin's men seized him by his hands and feet and hurled him out into space, but Li simply stretched out his legs until he felt firm ground beneath the soles of his feet, leaving his head level with the top of the cliff where his tormenters stood.

By this time the mandarin was foaming at the mouth with rage. He retired into his palace, and issued orders that Li should be burnt alive. A massive stake was driven into the ground in the palace courtyard, and a great pile of wood was heaped up round it. The courtyard was surrounded with a powerful armed guard, and people came running from all over the city in order to see Li burnt at the stake.

But Li the Second – the one who could not be burnt – managed to slip into the palace dungeon and change places with his long-legged brother just before the mandarin gave the order for the prisoner to be brought out and tied to the stake.

As soon as he was bound fast the executioners poured oil on the wood and set light to it. The flames crept higher and higher and clouds of smoke filled the air. Nothing could be seen of the unhappy boy tied to the stake in the midst of the smoke and flames, and many of the tender-hearted onlookers began to cry, they were so sorry for him.

In time the pile of wood was burnt up, the smoke died down, and the flames dwindled to a ruddy glow amongst the embers, and in the middle stood Li, still bound to the stake but unharmed and grinning from ear to ear!

The mandarin almost choked with rage. 'What can I do with this scoundrel?' he exclaimed. 'This cannot go on! It is ridiculous that I, a high and mighty mandarin, cannot deal with a common shepherd-boy!'

He thought things over, and ordered his men to tie an enormous boulder round Li's neck, take him out to sea in a ship, and throw him overboard.

The prison where Li awaited his fate was heavily guarded, but at the last moment Li the First – the Li who could drink the sea dry at a single gulp – managed to slip in and change places with his brother.

Early next morning Li was led aboard a ship, and the mandarin followed in a second ship with his entire court.

As soon as they were in the middle of the ocean an enormous boulder was tied round Li's neck, and at a sign from the cruel mandarin he was heaved overboard into the waves.

Li sank below the surface, and at once began to drink. It was not long before the mandarin noticed that the sea was becoming shallower, and he began to quake with fear. Soon the ship settled on the muddy ocean bed and heeled over on its side as the last of the sea-water disappeared, flinging the mandarin overboard.

Li untied the boulder from his neck and walked quietly to the shore, leaving the mandarin and his entire court floundering in the mud and slime. In no time the ocean waters were gushing out of Li's mouth to fill up the sea again.

The hard-hearted mandarin and his men-at arms were all drowned, for they were stuck fast in the muddy bed of the ocean. But all the people of that land were delighted to be free of the wicked tyrant, and sang grateful songs of praise to the five victorious brothers Li.

The Story of Caliph Stork

One warm afternoon the Caliph Hazid was reclining on his sofa in Baghdad. He had slumbered a little, for it was a particularly hot day, and he had woken much refreshed. He smoked a long rosewood pipe, and every now and then he took a sip of black coffee and stroked his long black beard. At about this hour he was always in a mild and affable mood, and so it was at this time every day that the

Grand Vizir would visit him to discuss affairs of state. He came that afternoon as usual, but he looked worried and unhappy, which was not at all usual.

'Why such a solemn face, Grand Vizir?' the caliph asked, taking the pipe from his mouth for a moment.

The Grand Vizir crossed his hands over his breast, bowed his head, and answered, 'My lord, I am sorry if I look a little worried, but there is a merchant down below who has so many wonderful things for sale that I am sad I have so little money to spare.'

For a long time the caliph had wanted to reward his vizir for his good service, so he sent a slave to bring the merchant to him. Before long the slave returned with the merchant, who was dark-featured and dressed in a tattered coat. He carried a wooden chest, which contained many beautiful things – pearls and rings, gold-mounted pistols and jewelled drinking-vessels, delicate combs and shimmering silks.

The caliph and his vizir examined everything with the greatest care, and the caliph finally bought a pair of magnificent pistols for the vizir and a carved ivory comb for the vizir's wife.

As the merchant was about to close the chest, the caliph noticed a tiny drawer, and asked to see what it contained. The merchant opened the drawer, and showed him a little box filled with a fine black powder, and a scrap of paper covered with writing which neither the caliph nor the vizir could read.

'These two articles I had from a trader,' said the merchant. 'He told me he had found them lying in the street in Mecca. I have no idea what they are. You can have them quite cheaply if you like.'

The caliph, who liked to have all sorts of curious and rare manuscripts in his library, even if he was unable to read them, bought the paper and the little box and dismissed the merchant. The caliph was eager to find out what the writing meant, and asked his vizir if there was no one in the city who could decipher it.

'My lord,' replied the vizir, 'there is a man who lives beside the great mosque. He is called Selim the Scholar, and he understands every tongue. If anyone can decipher this mysterious script, I am sure he can.'

So Selim the Scholar was sent for. 'Selim,' said the caliph, 'I hear you are a man of great learning. If you can tell me what is written upon this paper I will give you a new ceremonial coat. If not, you shall receive twelve strokes of the lash on your back, and twenty-five strokes of the cane on the soles of your feet, for you will not have lived up to your title of Selim the Scholar.'

Selim inclined his head, and said, 'It shall be as you wish, my lord.' With furrowed brow he pored over the scrap of paper, and exclaimed at last, 'I am certain it is Latin, my lord!'

'If it is really Latin,' replied the caliph, 'tell me what it says.' Selim began to translate slowly:

'You, who find this precious thing, praise Allah for his goodness. Whoever sniffs up a pinch of this powder, saying "Mutabor", shall have the power to turn himself into any animal he wishes, and to understand the language of animals. If he desires to return to his human form, he must bow three times towards the east, and again say "Mutabor". But beware! He who laughs while he occupies the form of an animal shall immediately lose all recollection of the magic word, and remain an animal for ever.'

The caliph was delighted with Selim the Scholar when he had finished reading these words. He made him swear not to tell a soul about it, gave him a magnificent new ceremonial coat, and dismissed him.

'That was indeed a good purchase,' he said to his vizir. 'What fun it will be! Come to me early tomorrow, and we will go out into the woods together, or down to the river. As soon as we have sniffed the powder from this box we shall be able to hear everything that is going on in the woods, in the fields, in the air, and in the waters of the river!'

Next morning Caliph Hazid and his vizir set off on their walk. The caliph had the little box of powder in his pocket, and after they had gone some distance from the palace he sent his retainers home, continuing alone with the vizir. At first they wandered through the palace gardens in the hope of finding some living creature on which to practise their art, but they found nothing. At last the vizir suggested that they should go to a marshy lake he knew, where water-birds were always to be found.

They crept quietly through the reeds to the edge of the lake, and saw a long-legged stork marching solemnly to and fro. It was looking for frogs, and was making strange rattling noises in its long throat from time to time. Meanwhile, high overhead, another stork wheeled and glided through the air.

'By my beard,' said the Grand Vizir, 'I wager that these two long-legged creatures are carrying on a most interesting conversation. How would you like to be a stork?'

'That is an excellent idea!' replied the caliph. 'But let us first remind ourselves what we must do in order to regain our human forms. Bow three times to the east, and say "Mutabor" – that's it! But, for heaven's sake, do not laugh, or we shall be well and truly lost!'

While the caliph was speaking the second stork began to come down to earth. Quickly he drew the little box from his pocket, took a pinch of the powder and sniffed it, offering some to the vizir at the same time. 'Mutabor!' they both cried together.

Their legs shrivelled up and turned red, their pointed yellow slippers turned into storks' feet, their arms became wings, their necks shot out above their shoulders, their beards vanished, and their bodies were soon covered in white feathers.

'What a beautiful beak you have, Grand Vizir!' said the caliph, as soon as he had recovered from his first astonishment. 'By the beard of the Prophet, I have seen nothing like it in my whole life.'

'Many thanks for your gracious compliment,' replied the vizir, making a bow. 'If I may say so, you look even more handsome as a stork than as a caliph. But let us not waste time. Let us see if we can understand the language of the storks.'

The second stork had that moment landed, and she was busy cleaning her feet with her beak and preening her breast feathers before paying her respects to the first stork. The two new storks hurried towards them, and were just in time to overhear the following conversation :

'Good morning, Madam Longshanks, you are out early this morning !'

'Good morning to you, dear Clipper-clapper. I have been out hunting my breakfast. Would you like to share a newt with me, or would you prefer a frog's leg?'

'Many thanks for your kind thought, but I am not hungry this morning. No, I am here for a very different reason. I have to dance before my father's guests this evening, and I must practise on my own.' And with these words the young stork marched sedately to an open space behind the reeds, and began a series of intricate movements, her legs, wings, and neck twisting and turning, waving and flapping, in a solemn dance.

To begin with, the caliph and his vizir were too astounded to speak but soon they could control themselves no longer, and a long cackle of laughter burst from their beaks.

'That is the funniest thing I have ever seen,' exclaimed the caliph when he had sufficiently recovered. 'What a pity the storks were frightened away by our laughter. We might have learned a great deal more by listening to them.'

Just then the vizir remembered that they ought not to have laughed whilst they were in the form of storks. He voiced his fear to the caliph, who said, 'Never mind – I would not have missed that for all the world, even if I do have to remain a stork! But surely you can remember the ridiculous word we had to repeat in order to become humans again?'

'We must turn towards the east, bow three times, and say, "Mu . . . Mu . . . Mu . . ."'

They turned to face the east and bowed three times till their beaks touched the ground, but no matter how long they thought, they could not remember the right word. 'Mu . . . Mu . . . Mu . . .' was as far as they could get.

Sadly they wandered through the fields, not knowing what to do. There was no means of escaping from their storks' bodies, nor could they very well return to the city and announce who they were, for who would believe that two common storks were the Caliph Hazid and his Grand Vizir!

For the first three days after their transformation they observed widespread signs of mourning and unrest in the city. But on the fourth day they saw a magnificent procession winding its way through the streets, to the accompaniment of pipes and drums and the clashing of cymbals, led by a man arrayed in a scarlet mantle and mounted on a snow-white horse. Half the population of Baghdad followed behind him, clapping and shouting, 'Long live Mirza, ruler of Baghdad!'

The two storks landed on the palace roof, and looked at each other. 'This is most suspicious,' said the Caliph Hazid to the Grand Vizir. 'I begin to guess why I have been bewitched. This man Mirza is the son of the powerful sorcerer Qazil Nur, who is my deadly enemy and swore to be revenged on me for some imagined affront. But let us not give up hope. Come with me, my faithful comrade in misfortune. Let us pay a visit to Medina, where we shall find the Prophet's grave. Perhaps the sanctity of that holy place will release us from our misfortune.'

So they took off from the palace roof, and flew towards Medina. The journey was more arduous than they had expected, for neither of them had flown so far before. Their wings felt weak and heavy from the long flight, and after a few hours the vizir groaned that he coud go no further. 'You are flying too fast,' he complained. 'Night is falling, and we should be looking for somewhere to spend the hours of darkness.'

The caliph agreed, and they dropped slowly down to the valley below, landing beside a ruined castle. They stalked wearily into the ruins, but they had not gone far before they stopped in their tracks, their feathers standing on end. 'My lord,' said the vizir, 'it may seem foolish for a stork – or for a Grand Vizir – to say so, but I am sure this place is haunted. I distinctly heard the sound of moaning!'

They stood motionless for a moment, and, sure enough, they heard again the sound of weeping and moaning. The caliph began to move towards it, but the vizir held him back, imploring him not to venture further into unknown dangers. The caliph insisted, however, and plunged down a dark, narrow corridor, until he came to a door. From behind it came the sound of sobbing. Gingerly he pushed the door open with his beak, and stood rooted to the spot with amazement.

In the dim starlight that filtered through a tiny grating

sat a brown owl. Huge tears filled her great round eyes, while from her beak came a dull moaning. As soon as the owl saw the storks, the moaning stopped and there was a sudden squawk of joy. Wiping the tears from her eyes with the tip of her speckled wing-feathers, the owl said, 'Welcome, storks! At last I have a good omen for my release! It was prophesied long ago that storks would bring me great happiness.'

As soon as the caliph had recovered from his astonishment, he bowed his long neck and replied, 'My dear owl, I can only assume from what you say that you are a comrade in misfortune. Far from being able to help you, however, we are powerless to help ourselves – as you will understand when you hear our sad story.'

When the Caliph Hazid had related his experiences, the

owl thanked him and said, 'My story is not much different from yours. My father is an Indian king, and I am his only daughter. I, too, was bewitched by the same sorcerer. One day he came to my father's court and demanded me in marriage for his son, Mirza. My father is quick-tempered, and he had him thrown out of the palace for his presumption. The wretch then disguised himself as a slave, and gave me a cup of ice-cool sherbet while I was resting in the gardens. It was this drink which transformed me into an owl. The wicked sorcerer brought me to this castle, and here I must stay until a man, of his own free will, asks me to marry him without having seen me in my true form. That was many moons ago. Now I pass my time in loneliness within these ruined walls. I cannot even see the beauties of nature, for I am blind during the hours of daylight, and the veil falls from my eyes only when the sun sinks below the horizon.' The owl finished speaking, and wiped her eyes once more with the tip of her wing.

The caliph remained deep in thought for some while before he spoke again. 'There must surely be some connection between your misfortune and ours,' he said at last.

'My lord,' said the owl, 'I am sure you are right, and I think I know how we may solve the problem. Every month the wicked sorcerer who has brought misfortune to us all visits these ruins to dine with a few chosen friends. It is possible that you might hear from them the word you need to release you from the spell, if you listen carefully.'

'Most wonderful princess!' exclaimed the caliph. 'When will he come, and where is the room where he will dine?'

'Not so fast,' said the owl, and paused for a moment. 'I

hope you will understand, but I can tell you only on one condition.'

'What is that?' cried the caliph. 'I will do whatever you wish!'

'My dearest wish, like yours, is to be set free, but that will be possible only if one of you will marry me.'

'Well, Grand Vizir,' whispered the caliph, 'will you ask her?'

'How can I, my lord?' replied the vizir, also in a whisper. 'You know that I am already married. Besides, I am old, while you are still young. You should be delighted to marry a beautiful young princess.'

'That is all very well,' sighed the caliph, drooping his wings, 'but who can tell if she is either young or beautiful?' But at last he agreed to ask the owl himself.

The owl was overjoyed, and confessed that the storks had arrived at the best possible time, for the sorcerer would almost certainly come with his friends that very night. She led the caliph and his vizir down a long, dark corridor, and after a while they saw a gleam of light ahead, where part of the wall had crumbled away. They crept up to the gap and looked down into a great banqueting-hall. Coloured lamps cast a strange light over a low table, round which eight men were sitting. The caliph quickly recognized one of these as the merchant who had sold him the black powder. He was telling his companions of his wicked deeds, which included the story of the Caliph Hazid and his Grand Vizir.

'What magic word did you give them?' asked all the other sorcerers.

'A really difficult Latin word,' he replied. 'Mutabor.'

The storks flapped their wings for joy, and the next

moment they were scurrying towards the open air so fast that the owl could hardly keep up with them. As soon as they were outside, the caliph turned to the owl and said, 'You have saved my life and the life of my friend, and have earned our eternal gratitude. Will you marry me?'

'I will,' replied the owl gently.

The two storks solemnly faced the rising sun, and bowed their long necks three times, so low that their beaks touched the ground. 'Mutabor!' they cried, and in a flash they were transformed into men.

But what was their amazement when they turned to the owl! For there stood a beautiful girl, her dark eyes sparkling and her long black hair flowing over her delicate shoulders.

Rejoicing in their freedom and good fortune the three set off for Baghdad, where the return of the caliph caused great astonishment, for his people had thought him dead. The hated usurper, Mirza, and the wicked sorcerer were speedily brought to judgment. With the aid of the magic powder the sorcerer was banished for ever to the ruined castle; but Mirza was turned into a stork and locked in an iron cage in the grounds of the caliph's palace.

For many years the Caliph Hazid lived happily with his beloved wife; but the happiest hours of all were those spent with his Grand Vizir each afternoon, when they recalled their adventures as storks.

Puss in Boots

A miller had three sons, and when he died he left them his mill, his donkey, and his cat. The eldest son took the mill, and the second the donkey, leaving the youngest with nothing but the cat. The poor lad was most dissatisfied with his miserable share. 'If my two brothers stay together they can easily earn an honest living,' he grumbled. 'The mill will grind, and the donkey can be used to fetch the grain and carry away the flour. But when I have eaten my cat and made a pair of mittens out of its skin, I shall be left to starve.'

But the cat had understood perfectly all that he had said, although he had pretended not to hear. Now he said, 'Do not worry, master. Give me a sack and have a pair of boots made for me, and I will soon show you that your share of the inheritance is by no means as poor as you think!'

The miller's son had little confidence in these words, but he certainly remembered that on many occasions he had admired the cat's skill and prowess at catching rats and mice. So he did as the creature asked.

When the boots were ready the cat pulled them on, flung the sack over his shoulder, holding the strings tightly between his paws, and set off for Cotton-tail Hill, which was always swarming with rabbits. When he arrived there he put some lettuce leaves in the bottom of the sack, and lay down beside it as if he were dead, waiting for some young rabbit, inexperienced in the wiles of this world, to venture inside the sack and sniff the lettuce leaves. He did not have long to wait before a small rabbit lolloped up and crawled into the sack. Quick as lightning the cat pulled the string tight, seized the rabbit, and quickly killed it.

Feeling very pleased with himself he went to the royal palace and demanded to speak to the king. He was granted admission, and when at last he stood before the king he made a sweeping bow, and said, 'Most gracious Majesty, my master, the Marquis of Carabas, sends you this rabbit with his most humble respects, and beseeches you to accept it.'

'Tell your master,' replied the king, 'that I am most grateful to him.'

Next day the cat hid in a corn-field, where he caught a brace of partridges. He took them to the palace, and again the king accepted the gift with pleasure, handing the cat a generous reward. So it went on for two or three months. Each day the cat delivered some game to the king, saying that it had been sent by his master, the Marquis of Carabas.

One day the cat discovered that the king intended to go for a drive in his carriage with his daughter, the princess. So he said to his master, 'Do not ask questions – just do as I tell you, and your fortune is made! All you have to do is to bathe at a certain bend in the river, which I shall point out to you, and I will see to the rest.'

The so-called Marquis of Carabas did exactly as the cat told him, without having any idea what the purpose was. While he was bathing, the king's carriage came bowling along, and the cat immediately began to call at the top of his voice, 'Help! Help! The Marquis of Carabas is drowning!'

The king stopped his carriage and put his head out of the window. He recognized at once the cat who had so often brought him game, and ordered his bodyguard to go to the rescue of the poor marquis. While his master was being hauled out of the river, the cat ran to the coach and told the king that thieves had stolen his master's clothes while he was bathing, although he had shouted at the top of his voice. (To tell the truth, the rascally cat had himself hidden the clothes under a stone, because they were all ragged and worn!)

The king was only too willing to show his gratitude to the kind marquis who had sent him so much game, and he ordered his footmen to fetch a suit of his own clothes for him. As the miller's son was a handsome young fellow, he looked a born nobleman in the fine clothes, with the result that the princess fell head over heels in love with him. The king meanwhile invited him to accompany them.

The cat was delighted with the success of his plan, and hurried on ahead. On the way he met harvesters cutting the corn, and said to them, 'Listen to me, good people. If the king asks you who owns this land, you must tell him it belongs to the Marquis of Carabas – otherwise you will all be chopped up into mincemeat!'

The king did indeed ask the harvesters who owned the land, and they all replied, 'The Marquis of Carabas, Your Majesty' – for the cat had put the fear of death into them.

'You have very fine lands, Marquis,' said the king.

'Quite good, Your Majesty,' replied the miller's son. 'The soil is excellent.'

The cat ran on in front, and came to some fields where harvesters were gathering and binding the sheaves. 'Listen to me, good people,' he said. 'If you do not tell the king that these fields belong to the Marquis of Carabas you will all be chopped up into little pieces.'

A few moments later the king drove by in his carriage,

and wanted to know who owned the fine fields. 'The Marquis of Carabas,' cried all the harvesters, and the king was delighted to hear it.

On the cat ran in front of the carriage, and warned everyone he met to give the same answer, with the result that the king was soon amazed at the wide extent of the lands of the Marquis of Carabas. At last the cat arrived at a magnificent castle, which belonged to the real owner of all this vast estate. He was a rich ogre who terrified the whole neighbourhood, and lived on human flesh.

Now the cat knew all about the ogre, but he was not afraid, and asked to see him immediately. For, he said, he could hardly pass the castle without calling to pay his respects. The ogre received him kindly, as ogres can when they are in the mood, and invited him to sit down.

'I have been told,' said the cat, 'that you are able to turn yourself into any living creature you like – even a lion or an elephant. Is that true?'

'Yes, it is,' roared the ogre, 'and I can soon prove it to you.'

Suddenly the ogre vanished, and in his place stood an enormous lion, swishing his tail and roaring so loudly that it seemed the roof would split. Scarcely had the ogre resumed his normal form than the cat jumped down from his chair, and pretended to be terrified, quaking in his boots.

'I have even been told,' he said, 'that you can turn yourself into the tiniest of creatures – for instance, a rat or a mouse – although I must confess that I find it very hard to believe.'

'You don't believe it?' exclaimed the ogre. 'I'll soon show you!' And that very instant the ogre turned himself into a tiny mouse, and began to scurry across the floor. That was just what the cat had been waiting for. With one leap he sprang on the mouse and gobbled it up!

At that very moment the king drew up to the castle. The cat had heard the royal carriage rattling over the drawbridge, and ran out to bid the king a hearty welcome to the castle of the Marquis of Carabas.

'Aha, Marquis!' cried the king. 'Why did you not tell us it was your castle? It is the most wonderful building I have ever seen. Will you permit us to see the inner rooms?'

The miller's son helped the princess out of the carriage, and they went together into the lofty dining-hall. There they found a splendid meal set out, which the ogre had prepared for himself. The king became more and more delighted with the castle and its wide domains, and when he had drunk five or six glasses of wine and had eaten a little meat he turned to the miller's son and said, 'Well, Marquis, how would you like to marry my daughter?'

The miller's son bowed low and accepted the king's gracious offer without a moment's hesitation. The marriage took place that very evening, and the miller's son and his wife lived happily in the castle for many, many years.

The cat soon became a great country gentleman, and chased mice only occasionally – for amusement.

The Swine-herd

There once lived a prince who possessed only a very small kingdom. But his ambitions were big enough, particularly when it came to choosing a bride.

You may think him impertinent when you hear that he went straight to the emperor's daughter and asked her to be his wife. But it was not as bold as it seems, for many hundreds of princesses would have been only too willing to marry him. The emperor's daughter, however, was of a different mind.

Now on the prince's father's grave there grew a rose-tree which was different from any other rose-tree, for it bloomed only once in every five years, and then it bore only a single rose. The rose, however, had such a wonderful scent that whoever smelt it for a single second would forget all his cares and troubles. The prince also possessed a nightingale which sang the sweetest songs, as if it knew by heart all the lovely melodies in the world. When the prince set out to woo the emperor's daughter, he placed both the rose and the nightingale in beautiful caskets and sent them to the princess.

The emperor had the gifts taken into the great hall where the princess was playing hide-and-seek amongst the pillars with her ladies-in-waiting. When she saw the beautiful silver caskets she clapped her hands for joy, and ran to see what was in them, for she loved receiving presents.

'I hope it's a kitten!' she cried – and took out the magnificent rose. The princess touched the delicate petals, and almost burst into tears. 'What a shame!' she cried. 'It's an ordinary rose!'

'What a shame!' repeated all the ladies-in-waiting. 'Just an ordinary rose!'

'Let us see what there is in the other casket before we show our displeasure,' said the emperor as he took out the nightingale. It sang so beautifully that you would have thought no one could possibly find fault with it.

'*Superbe, charmant*!' the ladies-in-waiting cried out, for they all babbled away perpetually in bad French.

'This bird,' remarked an elderly courtier, 'reminds me vividly of the late empress's musical box. It has exactly the same tone, the same style of singing!'

'Yes, yes, you're right!' said the emperor, and burst into tears.

'It isn't by any chance a *real* bird?' asked the princess.

'Yes, it is a real bird,' replied the messenger who had brought the presents.

'Then let it fly away!' she cried. And she was so angry that she would not even allow the prince to come in and see her.

The prince, however, was not to be so easily put off. He plastered his face with mud, pulled his cap well down over his eyes, and knocked at the palace door.

'Good day, Your Majesty,' he said. 'Have you any work for me in your palace?'

'I doubt it,' replied the emperor. 'I have already more servants than I need. But wait! I *am* looking for a swine-herd. We have so many pigs here to look after!'

So the prince became the imperial swine-herd. He was given a miserable little hovel beside the pig-sties to live in, and there he sat all day long, working. By the time evening came he had made a lovely little cooking-pot with tiny bells hanging from its rim. As soon as the pot came to the boil the little bells began to ring, and played:

'Oh, my darling Augustine,
All is lost, all is lost!'

But that was not all – no, not by any means! When a finger was held over the steam it was possible to smell everything that was cooking in every house in the whole city. That was much better than a mere rose!

Now it happened that the princess was passing by with her ladies-in-waiting when she heard the sweet tinkling of the tune. She was entranced, and stopped to listen. It was the only tune she could play.

'That is my song!' she cried. 'What a clever swine-herd he must be! Go and ask him if he will sell the cooking-pot.'

So one of the ladies-in-waiting had to go and ask, though she took care to pull her galoshes over her slippers before entering the swine-herd's hovel.

'How much will you take for the cooking-pot?' she asked.

'Ten kisses from the princess,' he replied.

'God forbid!' cried the lady-in-waiting.

'As you wish,' said the swine-herd. 'But she will have to do without my cooking-pot.'

'Well, what does he want?' asked the princess, when her lady-in-waiting returned.

'I hardly like to tell you!' stammered the lady-in-waiting. 'It is too frightful!'

'Then whisper it to me,' ordered the princess, and the lady-in-waiting did as she was told.

'What a brazen fellow he is!' exclaimed the princess,

and moved quicky on. Before they had gone far, however, they heard the little bells chime out again :

> 'Oh, my darling Augustine,
> All is lost, all is lost!'

'Go and ask him if ten kisses from any of my ladies-in-waiting would do instead,' said the princess.

'Oh no,' replied the swine-herd. 'Ten kisses from the princess or I keep my cooking-pot.'

'How frightful!' exclaimed the princess. 'Very well, I will do it – but you must all stand round me so that no one can see!'

So the ladies-in-waiting stood round the princess and spread out their skirts. The swine-herd received his ten kisses and the princess received her cooking-pot in exchange.

How pleased she was now! All the next day and throughout the evening the cooking-pot was continuously on the boil. There was not a house in the whole city where she did not know what was cooking, from the lord chamberlain's down to the cobbler's. The ladies-in-waiting danced and clapped their hands with delight.

'We know who is having broth and pancakes tonight! We know who is having meat puddings and who is having roast beef! How interesting!'

'Most interesting,' agreed the chief stewardess.

'Please don't give me away,' begged the princess. 'Remember I am the emperor's daughter!'

'God forbid!' said all the ladies-in-waiting. 'We'll not whisper a word!'

The swine-herd – that is to say, the prince – did not let a day pass by without inventing something new. One day he made a little barrel-organ, and as soon as it was turned it played all the waltzes, jigs and polkas that have ever been heard since the world began.

'How beautiful!' exclaimed the princess as she was passing by. 'I have never heard such wonderful dance music. Go and ask the swine-herd how much the instrument costs. But remember, no more kisses!'

Before long, however, the lady-in-waiting whom she had sent returned to say that he wanted a hundred kisses for it.

'He must be quite mad!' declared the princess, and went on her way. But she had not gone far before she stopped and said, 'I suppose I ought to do it for art's sake! I am the emperor's daughter after all. Go and tell him I will give him ten kisses, but the other ninety he must obtain from my ladies-in-waiting.'

'Oh, Madam! We cannot agree to that!' said the ladies.

'Nonsense!' said the princess. 'If I can kiss him, so can you. And remember, you depend on me for your board and lodging.' So the ladies-in-waiting had to return with this message.

'No,' said the swine-herd. 'I must have a hundred kisses from the princess, or I shall keep my barrel-organ.'

'Stand close round about me,' said the princess. So the ladies-in-waiting stood round in a circle, and the swine-herd began to kiss the princess.

'What is all that excitement down by the pig-sties?' exclaimed the emperor, who had strolled out on to the balcony at that moment. He rubbed his eyes, and put on his spectacles. 'Ah, as I thought! The ladies-in-waiting up to their nonsense again! I must go down and see what is going on this time!'

He quickly pulled on his slippers, and hurried downstairs. When he reached the courtyard, he crept up behind the little crowd as quietly as he could. The ladies-in-waiting were all far too busy counting the kisses to notice him, for they were determined that the princess should give neither more nor less than the hundred that had been agreed on. The emperor stretched up on the tips of his toes to see what was happening beyond the heads of the ladies-in-waiting.

'What is going on here?' he shouted, when he saw his daughter kissing the swine-herd. And he threw one of his slippers at them just as the swine-herd received his eighty-sixth kiss.

'Be off with you!' cried the emperor in a fury, and both the swine-herd and the princess were banished from the kingdom.

The princess stood and wept, while the swine-herd grumbled and scolded, and the rain streamed down. 'What a wretched creature I am!' she sobbed. 'If only I had married the prince when he asked me I should not be so unhappy now!'

Hearing these words, the swine-herd quietly slipped behind a tree, wiped the mud from his face, threw off his ragged clothes, and stepped out – looking so handsome in his princely tunic that the princess at once made a deep curtsey to him.

'Yes,' said the prince. 'You see now who you have refused. But I have come to despise you! You would have nothing to do with an honest prince – you even disdained my beautiful rose and my precious nightingale – yet you found time to kiss a swine-herd for the sake of a mere toy. What you suffer now is no more than you deserve!'

With these words he turned and went back to his own kingdom, slamming the castle gates in her face. All the princess could do was stay outside and sing:

> 'Oh, my darling Augustine,
> All is lost, all is lost!'

Some other Young Puffins

The Worst Witch
Jill Murphy

Mildred Hubble is the most disastrous dunce of all at Miss Cackle's training school for witches. But even the worst witch scores the occasional triumph!

The Shrinking of Treehorn
Florence Parry Heide

'Nobody shrinks,' declared Treehorn's father, but Treehorn *was* shrinking, and it wasn't long before even the unshakeable adults had to admit it.

Bad Boys
ed. Eileen Colwell

Twelve splendid stories about naughty boys, by favourite authors

A Gift from Winklesea
Helen Cresswell

Dan and Mary buy a beautiful stone like an egg as a present for their mother – and then it hatches out, into the oddest animal they ever saw.

Hide Till Daytime
Joan Phipson

The two children had been locked into the big department store by mistake at closing time, and whose were those prowling steps they could hear through the dark?

Tales of Joe and Timothy
Joe and Timothy Together
Dorothy Edwards

Friendly, interesting stories about two small boys living in different flats in a tall, tall house, and the good times they have together.

Secrets and Other Stories
Joan Wyatt

John often goes to stay with his 'country gran' who knows all about gingerbread men, blackberrying and being afraid of the dark. And at home he sometimes has to share his toys with his young cousin, though Grandad is usually there to keep the peace. A collection of warm, reassuring family stories for children.

Candy Floss *and* Impunity Jane
Rumer Godden

Two stories about dolls by an author who understands their feelings.

The Sawdust Secret
Jean Wills

How Sandy, John and Mike investigate the disappearance of some valuable antiques.

Time and Again Stories
Donald Bisset

It's rare to find nonsense stories as fresh and original as these. In Donald Bisset's world crows called Albert dream upside down and words get caught in telegraph wires.

Adventures of Sam Pig
Alison Uttley

Ten funny and magical stories about Alison Uttley's best-loved creation.

Dinner at Alberta's
Russell Hoban

Arthur the crocodile has extremely bad table manners – until he is invited to dinner at Alberta's.

Playtime Stories
Joyce Donoghue

Everyday children in everyday situations – these are stories for parents to read aloud and share with their children.

David and his Grandfather
Pamela Rogers

Three long stories about David and his kind, friendly Grandfather.

The Adventures of Uncle Lubin
W. Heath Robinson

The amazing adventures of good old Uncle Lubin in his search for his little nephew Peter, who has been stolen by the wicked Bag-bird. With the author's own unforgettable illustrations.